Careers in the
Face of Challenge

Careers in the Face of Challenge

Horatio Alger's *Telegraph Boy*

Edited and introduced by
Wallace Boston

WESTPHALIA PRESS
An imprint of Policy Studies Organization

Careers in the Face of Challenge
Horatio Alger's *Telegraph Boy*

Westphalia Press
An imprint of Policy Studies Organization
dgutierrezs@ipsonet.org

For information:
Westphalia Press
1527 New Hampshire Ave., N.W.
Washington, D.C. 20036

ISBN-13: 978-0944285954
ISBN-10: 0944285953

Updated material and comments on this edition can be found at the Policy Studies Organization website:
http://www.ipsonet.org/

Also from Westphalia Press

westphaliapress.org

CAREERS IN THE FACE OF CHALLENGE: HORATIO ALGER'S *THE TELEGRAPH BOY*

PREFACE TO THE NEW EDITION

Horatio Alger novels say a great deal about classic problems in education. The young people in Horatio Alger's novels always escape from poverty through hard work. By being newsboys or telegram delivery boys, they network and with true grit win out. But even the most ardent fans of Alger will admit that the odds were against them. In particular, they faced an uphill fight in getting an education. They were the support of their families, they had limited physical access to schools, and they had little money.

A century and more later, we have problems that in some ways are similar to the ones they faced. And perhaps we finally have some solutions. I will discuss a scenario or two, couch it with caveats, and acknowledge that technology changes so quickly that a new innovation could disrupt my disruption.

E

Die-hard opponents of change in higher education are not fans of online education. They argue that it is not as effective as face-to-face education despite evidence to the contrary. My response to the critics of online education is that the best teachers provide the best education regardless of medium. I was fortunate to have had great teachers and professors at the five schools and universities that I graduated from, but I also had a few not so great teachers. Online education is here to stay for a number of reasons: (1) it is a proven and acceptable medium of instruction, (2) online courses offered in asynchronous formats provide convenience for students who are unable or who do not want to attend classes (online or face-to-face) during more traditional times and at more traditional locations, (3) it provides a potential for scale in education, and (4) it provides a potential for lower cost education utilizing either technology, cost advantages due to the format (i.e., reduced/no cost of physical plant for classrooms, dormitories, cafeterias, athletic teams, etc.), scale, or any combination of the previous three.

Do I think that online education is going to continue to grow? Absolutely! Do I think that non-profits will accelerate the pace of growth of their online offerings? Absolutely! Do I think that some colleges will go out of business? Absolutely! Do I know who the successful colleges and universities will be and who the losers will be? No, I don't. However, I believe that one can make a few assumptions about the higher education landscape over the next few years.

First, the elite colleges will continue to thrive. They have the best resources including finances, brand, faculty, researchers, fund raising, and students. The value of their brand is buttressed by limiting the consumers of their product to a very small, elite group, with a backup group of consumers just as qualified as those admitted. Second, institutions with financial support beyond tuition and fees will survive assuming that they can continue to effectively offer a quality product for a cost that is covered by tuition, fees, and other sources of income. This group includes state schools and private non-profits with outside support and sizable endowments. Third, tuition dependent institutions with low enrollments and low endowments will find it difficult to survive. Moreover, the fixed cost model adopted by most of the traditional schools in this category will make survival difficult. Christensen recommends that these schools change their fixed cost model and embrace online courses/programs, priced at the margin. For the most part, these schools have ignored Christensen's advice. Lastly, institutions

G

with large online enrollments today will have to adapt to changes in the environment induced by technology including MOOCs, but probably not for the reasons that some imagine.

Higher education is under tremendous pricing pressures. The elite institutions can charge whatever they want, but the rest of the market is up for grabs. If a student is not able to obtain admission to a top 100 school, he is much more likely to examine all the factors including the cost of a degree at the institutions that accept him.

There is of course a lot of discussion about whether online education works. It can. Single courses are easy to design and offer for low cost, particularly if you can scale. But in my opinion, scaling and demonstrating quality learning outcomes for a diverse group of students is difficult to do. In fact, it's one of the reasons why our institution has capped the number of students in a course section at 25.

College, however, is and should be a lot more than a single course. The best online programs not only make the courses interesting but create online student commons to engage the student outside of the classroom. A college degree also implies that an individual has completed a prescribed curriculum that qualifies that individual for multiple career options and/or graduate studies. Institutions with

H

large online student populations will have to be mindful of the value proposition of their programs. Does it still pay for a student to complete many courses at the same institution or is the student better off to complete a number of free courses elsewhere? The quality of the programs, faculty and the career opportunities offered for their students/future graduates will aid those institutions in maintaining enrollments.

Those institutions with high tuition and a lower perceived value proposition will have trouble maintaining their enrollments given the new sources of competition. Presently, the traditional schools that are adding online enrollments are not providing lower cost alternatives and are relying on their brand appeal. Time will tell, but institutions that are adaptive and utilize technology in an effective manner should fare well. Possibly the Horatio Alger heros would have had a better chance of success in a world of online learning. Perhaps if Alger was writing today, his protagonists would be taking online courses as they tried to make their way in the world.

Wallace Boston, *American Public University*

"I come from your mother."

THE
TELEGRAPH BOY

BY

HORATIO ALGER, Jr.

AUTHOR OF

"STRONG AND STEADY," "BRAVE AND BOLD," "DO AND DARE,"
"STRIVE AND SUCCEED," "SLOW AND SURE,"
"FACING THE WORLD," ETC.

NEW YORK
THE NEW YORK BOOK COMPANY
1911

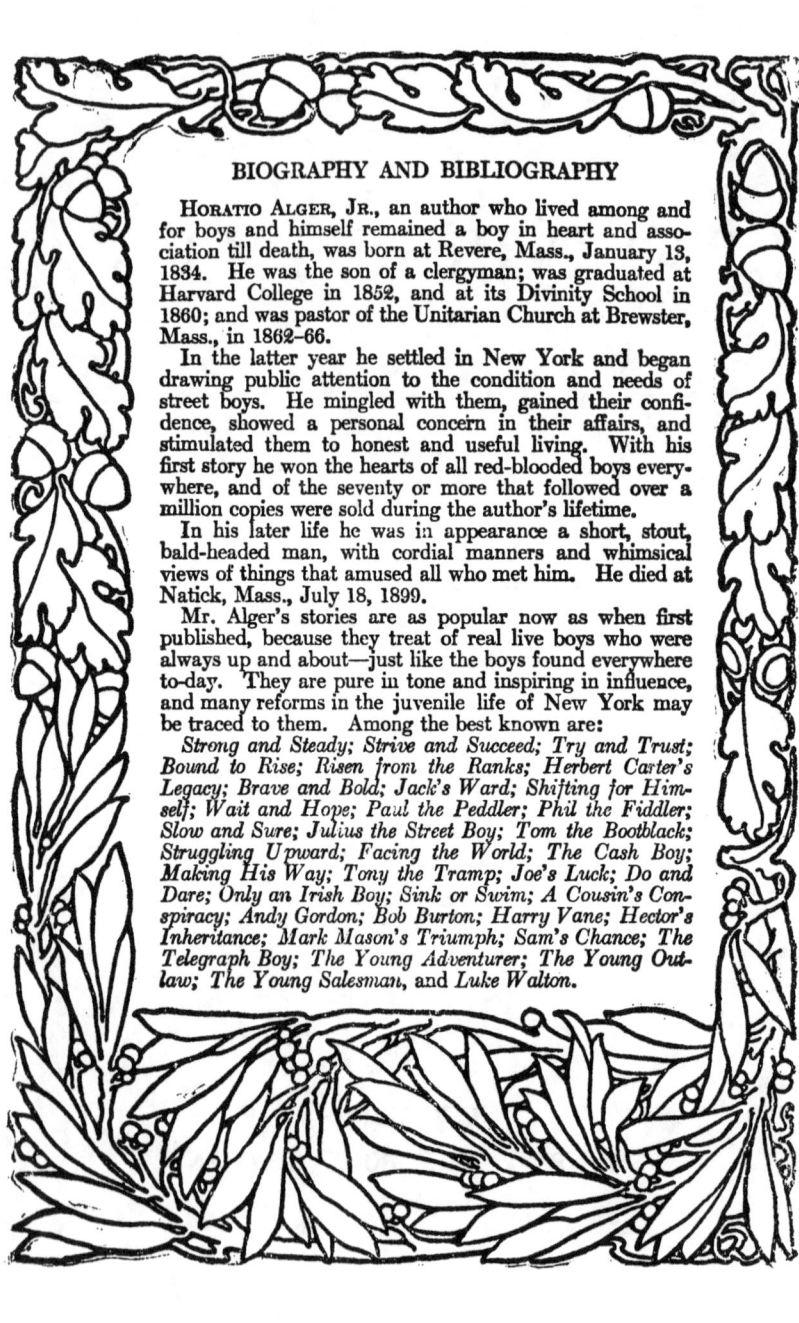

BIOGRAPHY AND BIBLIOGRAPHY

HORATIO ALGER, JR., an author who lived among and for boys and himself remained a boy in heart and association till death, was born at Revere, Mass., January 13, 1834. He was the son of a clergyman; was graduated at Harvard College in 1852, and at its Divinity School in 1860; and was pastor of the Unitarian Church at Brewster, Mass., in 1862–66.

In the latter year he settled in New York and began drawing public attention to the condition and needs of street boys. He mingled with them, gained their confidence, showed a personal concern in their affairs, and stimulated them to honest and useful living. With his first story he won the hearts of all red-blooded boys everywhere, and of the seventy or more that followed over a million copies were sold during the author's lifetime.

In his later life he was in appearance a short, stout, bald-headed man, with cordial manners and whimsical views of things that amused all who met him. He died at Natick, Mass., July 18, 1899.

Mr. Alger's stories are as popular now as when first published, because they treat of real live boys who were always up and about—just like the boys found everywhere to-day. They are pure in tone and inspiring in influence, and many reforms in the juvenile life of New York may be traced to them. Among the best known are:

Strong and Steady; Strive and Succeed; Try and Trust; Bound to Rise; Risen from the Ranks; Herbert Carter's Legacy; Brave and Bold; Jack's Ward; Shifting for Himself; Wait and Hope; Paul the Peddler; Phil the Fiddler; Slow and Sure; Julius the Street Boy; Tom the Bootblack; Struggling Upward; Facing the World; The Cash Boy; Making His Way; Tony the Tramp; Joe's Luck; Do and Dare; Only an Irish Boy; Sink or Swim; A Cousin's Conspiracy; Andy Gordon; Bob Burton; Harry Vane; Hector's Inheritance; Mark Mason's Triumph; Sam's Chance; The Telegraph Boy; The Young Adventurer; The Young Outlaw; The Young Salesman, and *Luke Walton.*

THE TELEGRAPH BOY

CHAPTER I

A YOUNG CARPET-BAGGER

"Twenty-five cents to begin the world with!" reflected Frank Kavanagh, drawing from his vest-pocket two ten-cent pieces of currency and a nickel. "That isn't much, but it will have to do."

The speaker, a boy of fifteen, was sitting on a bench in City-Hall Park. He was apparently about fifteen years old, with a face not handsome, but frank and good-humored, and an expression indicating an energetic and hopeful temperament. A small bundle, rolled up in a handkerchief, contained his surplus wardrobe. He had that day arrived in New York by a boat from Hartford, and meant to stay in the city if he could make a living.

Next to him sat a man of thirty-five, shabbily dressed, who clearly was not a member of any temperance society, if an inflamed countenance and red nose may be trusted. Frank Kavanagh's display of money attracted his attention, for, small as was the boy's capital, it was greater than his own.

"Been long in the city, Johnny?" he inquired.

"I only arrived to-day," answered Frank. "My name isn't Johnny, though."

"It's immaterial. Johnny is a generic term," said the stranger. "I suppose you have come here to make your fortune."

"I shall be satisfied with a living to begin with," said Frank.

"Where did you come from?"

"A few miles from Hartford."

"Got any relations there?"

"Yes—an uncle and aunt."

"I suppose you were sorry to leave them."

"Not much. Uncle is a pretty good man, but he's fond of money, and aunt is about as mean as they make 'em. They got tired of supporting me, and gave me money enough to get to New York."

"I suppose you have some left," said the stranger, persuasively.

"Twenty-five cents," answered Frank, laughing. "That isn't a very big capital to start on, is it?"

"Is that all you've got?" asked the shabbily dressed stranger, in a tone of disappointment.

"Every cent."

"I wish I had ten dollars to give you," said the stranger, thoughtfully.

"Thank you, sir; I wish you had," said Frank, his eyes resting on the dilapidated attire of his benevolent companion. Judging from that, he was not surprised that ten dollars exceeded the charitable fund of the philanthropist.

"My operations in Wall street have not been fortunate of late," resumed the stranger; "and I am in consequence hard up."

"Do you do business in Wall street?" asked Frank, rather surprised.

"Sometimes," was the reply. "I have lost heavily of late in Erie and Pacific Mail, but it is only temporary. I shall soon be on my feet again."

"I hope so, sir," said Frank, politely.

"My career has been a checkered one," continued the stranger. "I, too, as a mere boy, came up from the country to make my fortune. I embarked in trade, and was for a time successful. I resigned to get time to write a play—a comedy in five acts."

Frank regarded his companion with heightened respect. He was a boy of good education, and the author of a play in his eyes was a man of genius.

"Was it played?" he inquired.

"No; Wallack said it had too many difficult characters for his company, and the rest of the managers kept putting me off, while they were producing inferior plays. The American public will never know what they have lost. But, enough of this. Sometime I will read you the 'Mother-in-law,' if you like. Have you had dinner?"

"No," answered Frank. "Do you know where I can dine cheap?" he inquired.

"Yes," answered the stranger. "Once I boarded at the Astor House, but now I am forced, by dire necessity, to frequent cheap restaurants. Follow me."

"What is your name, sir?" asked Frank, as he rose from the bench.

"Montagu Percy," was the reply. "Sorry I haven't my card-case with me, or I would hand you my address. I think you said your name was not Johnny."

"My name is Frank Kavanagh."

"A very good name. 'What's in a name?' as Shakespeare says."

As the oddly assorted pair crossed the street, and walked down Nassau street, they attracted the attention of some of the Arabs who were lounging about Printing-House square.

"I say, country, is that your long-lost uncle?" asked a boot-black.

"No, it isn't," answered Frank, shortly.

Though he was willing to avail himself of Mr. Percy's guidance, he was not ambitious of being regarded as his nephew.

"Heed not their ribald scoffs," said Montagu Percy, loftily. "Their words pass by me 'like the idle wind,' which I regard not."

"Who painted your nose, mister?" asked another boy, of course addressing Frank's companion.

"I will hand you over to the next policeman," exclaimed Percy, angrily.

"Look out he don't haul you in, instead," retorted the boy.

Montagu Percy made a motion to pursue his tormentors, but desisted.

"They are beneath contempt," he said. "It is ever the lot of genius to be railed at by the ignorant and ignoble. They referred to my nose being red, but mistook the cause. It is a cutaneous eruption—the result of erysipelas."

"Is it?" asked Frank, rather mystified.

"I am not a drinking man—that is, I indulge myself but rarely. But here we are."

So saying, he plunged down some steps into a basement, Frank following him. Our hero found himself in a dirty apartment, provided with a bar, over which was a placard, inscribed:

"FREE LUNCH."

"How much money have you got, Frank?" inquired Montagu Percy.

"Twenty-five cents."

"Lunch at this establishment is free," said Montagu; "but you are expected to order some drink. What will you have?"

"I don't care for any drink except a glass of water."

"All right; I will order for you, as the rules of the establishment require it; but I will drink your glass myself. Eat whatever you like."

Frank took a sandwich from a plate on the counter and

ate it with relish, for he was hungry. Meanwhile his companion emptied the two glasses, and ordered another.

"Can you pay for these drinks?" asked the bartender, suspiciously.

"Sir, I never order what I cannot pay for."

"I don't know about that. You've been in here and taken lunch more than once without drinking anything."

"It may be so. I will make up for it now. Another glass, please."

"First pay for what you have already drunk."

"Frank, hand me your money," said Montagu.

Frank incautiously handed him his small stock of money, which he saw instantly transferred to the bartender.

"That is right, I believe," said Montagu Percy.

The barkeeper nodded, and Percy, transferring his attention to the free lunch, stowed away a large amount.

Frank observed with some uneasiness the transfer of his entire cash capital to the bartender; but concluded that Mr. Percy would refund a part after they went out. As they reached the street he broached the subject.

"I didn't agree to pay for both dinners," he said, uneasily.

"Of course not. It will be my treat next time. That will be fair, won't it?"

"But I would rather you would give me back a part of my money. I may not see you again."

"I will be in the Park to-morrow at one o'clock."

"Give me back ten cents, then," said Frank, uneasily. "That was all the money I had."

"I am really sorry, but I haven't a penny about me. I'll make it right to-morrow. Good-day, my young friend. Be virtuous and you will be happy."

Frank looked after the shabby figure ruefully. He felt that he had been taken in and done for. His small capital had vanished, and he was adrift in the streets of a strange city without a penny.

CHAPTER II

DICK RAFFERTY

"I've been a fool," said Frank to himself, in genuine mortification, as he realized how easily he had permitted himself to be duped. "I ought to have stayed in the country."

Even a small sum of money imparts to its possessor a feeling of independence, but one who is quite penniless feels helpless and apprehensive. Frank was unable even to purchase an apple from the snuffy old apple-woman who presided over the stand near by.

"What am I going to do?" he asked himself, soberly.

"What has become of your uncle?" asked a boot-black.

Looking up, Frank recognized one of those who had saluted Percy and himself on their way to the restaurant.

"He isn't my uncle," he replied, rather resentfully.

"You never saw him before, did you?" continued the boy.

"No, I didn't."

"That's what I thought."

There was something significant in the young Arab's tone, which led Frank to inquire, "Do you know him?"

"Yes, he's a dead-beat.

"A what?"

"A dead-beat. Don't you understand English?"

"He told me that he did business on Wall street."

The boot-black shrieked with laughter.

"He do business on Wall street!" he repeated. "You're jolly green, you are!"

Frank was inclined to be angry, but he had the good sense to see that his new friend was right. So he said good-humoredly, "I suppose I am. You see I am not used to the city."

"It's just such fellows as you he gets hold of," continued the boot-black. "Didn't he make you treat?"

"I may as well confess it," thought Frank. "This boy may help me with advice."

"Yes," he said aloud. "I hadn't but twenty-five cents, and he made me spend it all. I haven't a cent left."

"Whew!" ejaculated the other boy. "You're beginnin' business on a small capital."

"That's so," said Frank. "Do you know any way I can earn money?"

Dick Rafferty was a good-natured boy, although rough, and now that Frank had appealed to him for advice he felt willing to help him, if he could.

"What can you do?" he asked, in a business-like tone. "Have you ever worked?"

"Yes," answered Frank.

"What can you do?"

"I can milk cows, hoe corn and potatoes, ride horse to plow, and——"

"Hold up!" said Dick. "All them things ain't goin' to do you no good in New York. People don't keep cows as a reg'lar thing here."

"Of course I know that."

"And there ain't much room for plantin' corn and potatoes. Maybe you could get a job over in Jersey."

"I'd rather stay in New York. I can do something here."

"Can you black boots, or sell papers?"

"I can learn."

"You need money to set up in either of them lines," said Dick Rafferty.

"Would twenty-five cents have been enough?" asked Frank.

"You could have bought some evening papers with that."

"I wish somebody would lend me some money," said

Frank; "I'd pay it back as soon as I'd sold my papers. I was a fool to let that fellow swindle me."

"That's so," assented Dick; "but it's no good thinkin' of that now. I'd lend you the money myself, if I had it; but I've run out my account at the Park Bank, and can't spare the money just at present."

"How long have you been in business?" asked Frank.

"Ever since I was eight years old; and I'm goin' on fifteen now."

"You went to work early."

"Yes, I had to. Father and mother both died, and I was left to take care of myself."

"You took care of yourself when you were only eight years old?" asked Frank, in surprise.

"Yes."

"Then I ought to make a living, for I am fifteen—a year older than you are now."

"Oh, you'll get along when you get started," said Dick, encouragingly. "There's lots of things to do."

"Is there anything to do that doesn't require any capital?" inquired Frank, anxiously.

"Yes, you can smash baggage."

"Will people pay for that?" asked Frank, with a smile.

"Of course they will. You jest hang round the ferries and steamboat landin's, and when a chap comes by with a valise or carpet-bag, you jest offer to carry it, that's all."

"Is that what you call smashing baggage?"

"Of course. What did you think it was?"

Frank evaded answering, not caring to display his country ignorance.

"Do you think I can get a chance to do that?" he asked.

"You can try it and see."

"I came in by the Hartford boat myself, to-day," said Frank. "If I'd thought of it, I would have begun at once."

"Only you wouldn't have knowed the way anywhere, and if a gentleman asked you to carry his valise to any hotel you'd have had to ask where it was."

"So I should," Frank admitted.

"I'll show you round a little, if you want me to," said Dick. "I shan't have anything to do for an hour or two."

"I wish you would."

So the two boys walked about in the lower part of the city, Dick pointing out hotels, public buildings, and prominent streets. Frank had a retentive memory, and stored away the information carefully. Penniless as he was, he was excited and exhilarated by the scene of activity in which he was moving, and was glad he was going to live in it, or to attempt doing so.

"When I am used to it I shall like it much better than the country," he said to Dick. "Don't you?"

"I don't know about that," was the reply. "Sometimes I think I'll go West—a lot of boys that I know have gone there."

"Won't it take a good deal of money to go?" asked Frank.

"Oh, there's a society that pays boys' expenses, and finds 'em nice homes with the farmers. Tom Harrison, one of my friends, went out six weeks ago, and he writes me that it's bully. He's gone to some town in Kansas."

"That's a good way off."

"I wouldn't mind that. I'd like ridin' in the cars."

"It would be something new to you; but I've lived in the country all my life; I'd rather stay here awhile."

"It's just the way a feller feels," said Dick philosophically. "I've bummed around so much I'd like a good, stiddy home, with three square meals a day and a good bed to sleep on."

"Can't you get that here?" asked Frank.

"Not stiddy. Sometimes I don't get but one square meal a day."

Frank became thoughtful. Life in the city seemed more precarious and less desirable than he anticipated.

"Well, I must go to work again," said Dick, after a while.

"Where are you going to sleep to-night?" asked Frank.

"I don't know whether I'd better sleep at the Astor House or Fifth avenue," said Dick.

Frank looked perplexed.

"You don't mean that, do you?" he asked.

"Of course I don't. You're too fresh. Don't get mad," he continued good-naturedly, seeing the flush on Frank's cheek. "You'll know as much about the city as I do before long. I shall go to the Newsboys' Lodgin' House, where I can sleep for six cents."

"I wish I had six cents," said Frank. "If I could only get work I'd soon earn it. You can't think of anything for me to do, can you?"

Dick's face lighted up.

"Yes," he said, "I can get you a job, though it ain't a very good one. I wonder I didn't think of it before."

"What is it?" asked Frank, anxiously.

"It's to go round with a blind man, solicitin' contributions."

"You mean begging?"

"Yes; you lead him into stores and countin' rooms, and he asks for money."

"I don't like it much," said Frank, slowly, "but I must do something. After all, it'll be he that's begging, not I."

"I'll take you right round where he lives," said Dick. "Maybe he'll go out this evenin'. His other boy give him the slip, and he hasn' got a new one yet."

CHAPTER III

FRANK FINDS AN EMPLOYER

A STONE's throw from Centre street stands a tall tene-ment-house, sheltering anywhere from forty to fifty fam-ilies in squalid wretchedness. The rent which each family pays would procure a neat house in a country town, with perhaps a little land beside; but the city has a mysterious fascination for the poorer classes, and year after year many who might make the change herd together in con-tracted and noisome quarters, when they might have their share of light and space in country neighborhoods.

It was in front of this tenement-house that Dick halted, and plunged into a dark entrance, admonishing Frank to follow. Up creaking and dilapidated staircases to the fourth floor the boys went.

"Here we are," said Dick, panting a little from the rapidity of his ascent, and began a vigorous tattoo on a door to the left.

"Is this where the blind gentleman lives?" asked Frank, looking around him dubiously.

"He isn't much of a gentleman to look at," said Dick, laughing. "Do you hear him?"

Frank heard a hoarse growl from the inside, which might have been "Come in." At any rate, Dick chose so to interpret it, and opened the door.

The boys found themselves in a scantily furnished room, with a close, disagreeable smell pervading the atmosphere. In the corner was a low bedstead, on which lay a tall man, with a long, gray beard, and a disagreeable, almost re-pulsive, countenance. He turned his eyes, which, contrary to Frank's expectations, were wide open, full upon his visitors.

"What do you want?" he asked querulously. "I was asleep, and you have waked me up."

"Sorry to disturb you, Mr. Mills," said Dick; "but I come on business."

"What business can you have with me?" demanded the blind man. "Who are you?"

"I am Dick Rafferty. I black boots in the Park," replied Dick.

"Well, I haven't got any money to pay for blacking boots."

"I didn't expect you had. I hear your boy has left you."

"Yes, the young rascal! He's given me the slip. I expect he's robbed me, too; but I can't tell, for I'm blind."

"Do you want a new boy?"

"Yes; but I can't pay much. I'm very poor. I don't think the place will suit you."

"Nor I either," said Dick, frankly. "I'd rather make a living outside. But I've got a boy with me who has just come to the city, and is out of business. I guess he'll engage with you."

"What's his name? Let him speak for himself."

"My name is Frank Kavanagh," said our hero, in a clear, distinct voice.

"How old are you?"

"Fifteen."

"Do you know what your duties will be?"

"Yes; Dick has told me."

"I told him you'd want him to go round on a collecting tour with you every day," said Dick.

"That isn't all. You'll have to buy my groceries and all I need."

"I can do that," said Frank, cheerfully, reflecting that this would be much more agreeable than accompanying the old man round the streets.

"Are you honest?" queried the blind man, sharply.

Frank answered, with an indignant flush, " I never stole a cent in my life."

" I supposed you'd say that," retorted the blind man, with a sneer. " They all do; but a good many will steal for all that."

" If you're afraid I will, you needn't hire me," said Frank, independently.

" Of course I needn't," said Mills, sharply; " but I am not afraid. If you take any of my money I shall be sure to find it out, if I am blind."

" Don't mind him, Frank," said Dick, in a low voice.

" What's that?" asked the blind man, suspiciously. " What are you two whispering about?"

" I told Frank not to mind the way you spoke," said Dick.

" Why not?"

" Because, if he's honest, it don't matter."

" That's so," said Mills, partially satisfied. " Now what pay do you expect?"

" I'll leave that to you," said our hero, who felt that he was not in a position to make terms.

This answer seemed to please the blind man.

" Yes, yes, that is right. I can tell better in a week what I can afford to pay you. I'll let you come and try how you suit me."

" Am I to stay here?" asked Frank.

" Yes; there's a bed in the other room. Go in and see it."

The boys entered an inner room, where there was a heap of rags on the floor, and no other article.

" There's your bed, Frank," said Dick, pointing to the rags.

" Have I got to sleep there?" asked Frank, in a tone of dissatisfaction.

" Oh, it'll be comfortable enough," said Dick, whose street life had cured him of fastidiousness, if he had ever been troubled by that feeling. "If you'd slept on wharves and in empty wagons as often as I have you wouldn't mind that."

"I guess I can stand it," said Frank, stifling his dissatisfaction; "but I've always slept in a bed."

"Oh, you'll like it well enough," said Dick, carelessly. "Well, I must leave you now, I've got to earn my supper."

"Do you want me now, sir?" asked Frank of his new master.

"Yes; I want you to get me something to eat. You can go with this boy, and he'll tell you where to get it."

"What shall I buy, sir?"

"Buy a loaf of bread at the baker's, and a bottle of ale."

"Yes, sir."

"You can pay for it, and I will pay you when you get back."

"I have no money," said Frank, embarrassed.

"No money!" snarled the blind man.

"No, sir; I only brought twenty-five cents with me, and that I have spent."

"Your friend will lend you some, then."

"Not much," answered Dick, laughing. "I'm dead-broke. Haven't you got any money, Mr. Mills?"

"I have a little," grumbled the blind man; "but this boy may take it, and never come back."

"If you think so," said Frank, proudly, "you'd better engage some other boy."

"No use; you're all alike. Wait a minute, and I'll give you some money."

He drew from his pocket a roll of scrip, and handed one to Frank.

"I don't think that will be enough," said Frank. "It's only five cents."

"Are you sure it isn't a quarter?" grumbled Mills.

"Yes, sir."

"What do you say—you, Dick?"

"It's only five cents, sir."

"Is that twenty-five?"

"Yes, sir."

"Then take it, and mind you don't loiter."

"Yes, sir."

"And be sure to bring back the change."

"Of course I will," said Frank, indignantly, resenting his employer's suspicion.

"What do you think of him, Frank?" asked Dick, as they descended the stairs.

"I don't like him at all, Dick," said Frank, decidedly. "I wish I could get something else to do."

"You can, after a while. As you have no capital you must take what you can get now."

"So I suppose; but I didn't come to the city for this."

"If you don't like it you can leave in a few days."

This Frank fully resolved to do at the first favorable opportunity.

Dick showed him where he could buy the articles he was commissioned to purchase; and Frank, after obtaining them, went back to the tenement-house.

Mills scrupulously demanded the change, and put it back into his pocket. Then he made Frank pour out the ale into a glass. This he drank with apparent zest, but offered none to Frank.

"Ale isn't good for boys," he said. "You can cut the bread, and eat two slices. Don't cut them too thick."

The blind man ate some of the bread himself, and then requested Frank to help him on with his coat and vest.

"I haven't taken any money to-day," he said. "I must try to collect some, or I shall starve. It's a sad thing to be blind," he continued, his voice changing to a whine.

"You don't look blind," said Frank, thoughtfully. "Your eyes are open."

"What if they are?" said Mills, testily. "I cannot

see. When I go out I close them because the light hurts them."

Led by Frank, the blind man descended the stairs, and emerged into the street.

CHAPTER IV

"PITY THE BLIND"

"WHERE shall I lead you?" asked Frank.

"To Broadway first. Do you know Broadway?"

"Yes, sir."

"Be careful when we cross the street, or you will have me run over."

"All right, sir."

"If any one asks you about me, say I am your uncle."

"But you are not."

"What difference does that make, you little fool?" said the blind man, roughly. "Are you ashamed to own me as your uncle?"

Frank felt obliged, out of politeness, to say "No"; but in his own mind he was not quite sure whether he would be willing to acknowledge any relationship to the disagreeable old man whom he was leading.

They reached Broadway, and entered a store devoted to gentlemen's furnishing goods.

"Charity for a poor blind man!" whined Mills, in the tone of a professional beggar.

"Look here, old fellow, you come in here too often," said a young salesman. "I gave you five cents yesterday."

"I didn't know it," said Mills. "I am a poor blind man. All places are alike to me."

"Then your boy should know better. Nothing for you to-day."

Frank and his companion left the store.

In the next they were more fortunate. 'A nickel was bestowed upon the blind mendicant.

"How much is it?" asked Mills, when they were on the sidewalk.

"Five cents, sir."

"That's better than nothing, but we ought to do better. It takes a good many five-cent pieces to make a dollar. When you see a well-dressed lady coming along, tell me."

Frank felt almost as much ashamed as if he were himself begging, but he must do what was expected of him. Accordingly he very soon notified the blind man that a lady was close at hand.

"Lead me up to her, and say, ' Can you spare something for my poor, blind uncle '? "

Frank complied in part, but instead of " poor, blind uncle " he said " poor, blind man." Mills scowled, as he found himself disobeyed.

"How long has he been blind?" asked the lady, sympathetically.

"For many years," whined Mills.

"Is this your boy?"

"Yes, ma'am; he is my young nephew, from the country."

"You are fortunate in having him to go about with you."

"Yes, ma'am; I don't know what I should do without him."

"Here is something for you, my good man," said the lady, and passed on.

"Thank you, ma'am. May Heaven bless you!"

"How much is it?" he asked quickly, when the lady was out of hearing.

"Two cents," answered Frank, suppressing with difficulty an inclination to laugh.

"The mean jade! I should like to wring her neck!" muttered Mills. " I thought it was a quarter, at least."

In the next store they did not meet a cordial reception.

"Clear out, you old humbug!" shouted the proprietor, who was in ill-humor. "You ought to be put in the penitentiary for begging about the streets."

"I pray to God that you may become blind yourself," said Mills, passionately.

"Out of my store, or I'll have you arrested, both of you!" said the angry tradesman. "Here, you boy, don't you bring that old fraud in this store again, if you know what's best for yourself."

There was nothing to do but to comply with this peremptory order.

"He's a beast!" snarled Mills; "I'd like to put his eyes out myself."

"You haven't got a very amiable temper," thought Frank. "I wouldn't like to be blind; but even if I were, I would try to be pleasanter."

Two young girls, passing by, noticed the blind man. They were soft-hearted, and stopped to inquire how long he had been blind.

"Before you were born, my pretty maid," said Mills, sighing.

"I have an aunt who is blind," said one of the girls; "but she is not poor, like you."

"I am very poor," whined Mills; "I have not money enough to pay my rent, and I may be turned out into the street."

"How sad!" said the young girl, in a tone of deep sympathy. "I have not much money, but I will give you all I have."

"May God bless you, and spare your eyes!" said Mills, as he closed his hand upon the money.

"How much is it?" he asked as before, when they had passed on.

"Twenty-five cents," said Frank.

"That is better," said Mills, in a tone of satisfaction.

For some time afterwards all applications were refused; in some cases roughly.

"Why don't you work?" asked one man, bluntly.

"What can I do?" asked Mills.

"That's your lookout. Some blind men work. I suppose you would rather get your living by begging."

"I would work my fingers to the bone if I could only see," whined Mills.

"So you say; but I don't believe it. At any rate, that boy of yours can see. Why don't you set him to work?"

"He has to take care of me."

"I would work if I could get anything to do," said Frank.

As he spoke, he felt his hand pressed forcibly by his companion, who did not relish his answer.

"I cannot spare him," he whined. "He has to do everything for me."

When they were again in the street, Mills demanded, roughly, "What did you mean by saying that?"

"What, sir?"

"That you wanted to go to work."

"Because it is true."

"You are at work; you are working for me," said Mills.

"I would rather work in a store, or an office, or sell papers."

"That wouldn't do me any good. Don't speak in that way again."

The two were out about a couple of hours, and very tiresome Frank found it. Then Mills indicated a desire to go home, and they went back to the room in the old tenement-house. Mills threw himself down on the bed in the corner, and heaved a sigh of relief.

"Now, boy, count the money we have collected," he said.

"There's ninety-three cents," Frank announced.

"If I had known it was so near a dollar we would have stayed a little longer. Now, get me my pipe."

"Where is it, sir?"

"In the cupboard. Fill it with tobacco, and light it."

"Are you not afraid of setting the bedding on fire, sir?"

"Mind your own business. If I choose to set it on fire, I will," snarled Mills.

"Very well, sir; I thought I'd mention it."

"You have mentioned it, and you needn't do it again."

"What a sweet temper you've got!" thought Frank.

He sat down on a broken chair, and, having nothing else to do, watched his employer. "He looks very much as if he could see," thought Frank; for Mills now had his eyes wide open.

"What are you staring at me for, boy?" demanded his employer, rather unexpectedly.

"What makes you think I am staring at you, sir?" was Frank's natural question. "I thought you couldn't see."

"No more I can, but I can tell when one is staring at me. It makes me creep all over."

"Then I'll look somewhere else."

"Would you like to do some work, as you said?"

"Yes, sir."

"Then take twenty-five cents, and buy some evening papers and sell them; but mind you bring the money to me."

"Yes, sir," said Frank, with alacrity.

Anything he thought would be better than sitting in that dull room with so disagreeable a companion.

"Mind you don't run off with the money," said the blind man, sharply. "If you do I'll have you put in the Tombs."

"I don't mean to run away with the money," retorted Frank, indignantly.

"And when you've sold the papers, come home."

"Yes, sir."

With a feeling of relief, Frank descended the stairs and directed his steps to the Park, meaning to ask Dick Rafferty's advice about the proper way to start in business as a newsboy.

CHAPTER V

FRANK THROWS UP HIS SITUATION

FRANK found his friend on Park Row, and made known his errand.

"So old Mills wants you to sell papers for his benefit, does he?"

"Yes, but I'd rather do it than to stay with him."

"How much has he agreed to pay you?"

"That isn't settled yet."

"You'd better bring him to the point, or he won't pay you anything except board and lodging, and mighty mean both of them will be."

"I won't say anything about it the first day," said Frank. "What papers shall I buy?"

"It's rather late. You'd better try for Telegrams."

Frank did so, and succeeded in selling half a dozen, yielding a profit of six cents. It was not a brilliant beginning, but he was late in the field, and most had purchased their evening papers. His papers sold, Frank went home and announced the result.

"Umph!" muttered the blind man. "Give me the money."

"Here it is, sir."

"Have you given me all?" sharply demanded Mills.

"Of course I have," said Frank, indignantly.

"Don't you be impudent, or I will give you a flogging," said the blind man, roughly.

"I am not used to be talked to in that way," said Frank, independently.

"You've always had your own way, I suppose," snarled Mills.

"No, I haven't; but I have been treated kindly."

"You are only a boy, and I won't allow you to talk back to me. Do you hear?"

"Yes."

"Then take care to remember."

"You've got a sweet disposition," thought Frank. "I won't stay with you any longer than I am obliged to."

Several days passed without bringing any incidents worth recording. Frank took a daily walk with the blind man, sometimes in the morning, sometimes in the afternoon. These walks were very distasteful to him. The companion of a beggar, he felt as if he himself were begging. He liked better the time he spent in selling papers, though he reaped no benefit himself. In fact, his wages were poor enough. Thus far his fare had consisted of dry bread with an occasional bun. He was a healthy, vigorous boy, and he felt the need of meat, or some other hearty food, and ventured to intimate as much to his employer.

"So you want meat, do you?" snarled Mills.

"Yes, sir; I haven't tasted any for a week."

"Perhaps you'd like to take your meals at Delmonico's?" sneered the blind man.

Frank was so new to the city that this well-known name did not convey any special idea to him, and he answered "Yes."

"That's what I thought!" exclaimed Mills, angrily. "You want to eat me out of house and home."

"No, I don't; I only want enough food to keep up my strength."

"Well, you are getting it. I give you all I can afford."

Frank was inclined to doubt this. He estimated that

what he ate did not cost his employer over six or eight cents a day, and he generally earned for him twenty to thirty cents on the sale of papers, besides helping him to collect about a dollar daily from those who pitied his blindness.

He mentioned his grievance to his friend, Dick Rafferty.

"I'll tell you what to do," said Dick.

"I wish you would."

"Keep some of the money you make by selling papers, and buy a square meal at an eatin' house."

"I don't like to do that; it wouldn't be honest."

"Why wouldn't it?"

"I am carrying on the business for Mr. Mills. He supplies the capital."

"Then you'd better carry it on for yourself."

"I wish I could."

"Why don't you?"

"I haven't any money."

"Has he paid you any wages?"

"No."

"Then make him."

Frank thought this a good suggestion. He had been with Mills a week, and it seemed fair enough that he should receive some pay besides a wretched bed and a little dry bread. Accordingly, returning to the room, he broached the subject.

"What do you want wages for?" demanded Mills, displeased.

"I think I earn them," said Frank, boldly.

"You get board and lodging. You are better off than a good many boys."

"I shall want some clothes, some time," said Frank.

"Perhaps you'd like to have me pay you a dollar a day," said Mills.

"I know you can't afford to pay me that. I will be satisfied if you will pay me ten cents a day," replied Frank.

Frank reflected that, though this was a very small sum, in ten days it would give him a dollar, and then he would feel justified in setting up a business on his own account, as a newsboy. He anxiously awaited an answer.

"I will think of it," said the blind man evasively, and Frank did not venture to say more.

The next day, when Mills, led by Frank, was on his round, the two entered a cigar-store. Frank was much surprised when the cigar-vender handed him a fifty-cent currency note. He thought there was some mistake.

"Thank you, sir," he said; "but did you mean to give me fifty cents?"

"Yes," said the cigar-vender, laughing; "but I wouldn't have done it, if it had been good."

"Isn't it good?"

"No, it's a counterfeit, and a pretty bad one. I might pass it, but it would cost me too much time and trouble."

Frank was confounded. He mechanically handed the money to Mills, but did not again thank the giver. When they returned to the tenement-house, Mills requested Frank to go to the baker's for a loaf of bread.

"Yes, sir."

"Here is the money."

"But that is the counterfeit note," said Frank, scrutinizing the bill given him.

"What if it is?" demanded Mills, sharply.

"It won't pass."

"Yes, it will, if you are sharp."

"Do you want me to pass counterfeit money, Mr. Mills?"

"Yes, I do; I took it, and I mean to get rid of it."

"But you didn't give anything for it."

"That's neither here nor there. Take it, and offer it to the baker. If he won't take it, go to another baker with it."

"I would rather not do it," said Frank, firmly.

"Rather not!" exclaimed Mills, angrily. "Do you pretend to dictate to me?"

"No, I don't, but I don't mean to pass any counterfeit money for you or any other man," said Frank, with spirit.

Mills half rose, with a threatening gesture, but thought better of it.

"You're a fool," said he. "I suppose you are afraid of being arrested; but you have only to say that I gave it to you, and that I am blind, and couldn't tell it from good money."

"But you know that it is bad money, Mr. Mills."

"What if I do? No one can prove it. Take the money, and come back as quick as you can."

"You must excuse me," said Frank, quietly, but firmly.

"Do you refuse to do as I bid you?" demanded Mills, furiously.

"I refuse to pass counterfeit money."

"Then, by Heaven, I'll flog you!"

Mills rose and advanced directly toward Frank, with his eyes wide open. Fortunately our hero was near the door, and, quickly opening it, darted from the room, pursued by Mills, his face flaming with wrath. It flashed upon Frank that no blind man could have done this. He decided that the man was a humbug, and could see a little, at all events. His blindness was no doubt assumed to enable him to appeal more effectively to the sympathizing public. This revelation disgusted Frank. He could not respect a man who lived by fraud. Counterfeit or no counterfeit, he decided to withdraw at once and forever from the service of Mr. Mills.

His employer gave up the pursuit before he reached the street. Frank found himself on the sidewalk, free and emancipated, no richer than when he entered the service of the blind man, except in experience.

"I haven't got a cent," he said to himself, "but I'll get along somehow."

CHAPTER VI

FRANK GETS A JOB

THOUGH Frank was penniless he was not cast down. He was tolerably familiar with the lower part of the city, and had greater reliance on himself than he had a week ago. If he had only had capital to the extent of fifty cents he would have felt quite at ease, for this would have set him up as a newsboy.

"I wonder if I could borrow fifty cents of Dick Rafferty," considered Frank. "I'll try, at any rate."

He ran across Dick in City Hall Park. That young gentleman was engaged in pitching pennies with a brother professional.

"I say, Dick, I want to speak to you a minute," said Frank.

"All right! Go ahead!"

"I've lost my place."

Dick whistled.

"Got sacked, have you?" he asked.

"Yes; but I might have stayed."

"Why didn't you?"

"Mills wanted me to pass a counterfeit note, and I wouldn't."

"Was it a bad-looking one?"

"Yes."

"Then you're right. You might have got nabbed."

"That wasn't the reason I refused. If I had been sure there'd have been no trouble I wouldn't have done it."

"Why not?" asked Dick, who did not understand our hero's scruples.

"Because it's wrong."

Dick shrugged his shoulders.

"I guess you belong to the church," he said.

"No, I don't; what makes you think so?"

"Oh, 'cause you're so mighty particular. I wouldn't mind passing it if I was sure I wouldn't be cotched."

"I think it's almost as bad as stealing to buy bread, or anything else, and give what isn't worth anything for it. You might as well give a piece of newspaper."

Though Frank was unquestionably right he did not succeed in making a convert of Dick Rafferty. Dick was a pretty good boy, considering the sort of training he had had; but passing bad money did not seem to him objectionable, unless "a fellow was cotched," as he expressed it.

"Well, what are you going to do now?" asked Dick, after a pause.

"I guess I can get a living by selling papers."

"You can get as good a livin' as old Mills gave you. You'll get a better bed at the lodgin'-house than that heap of rags you laid on up there."

"But there's one trouble," continued Frank, "I haven't any money to start on. Can you lend me fifty cents?"

"Fifty cents!" repeated Dick. "What do you take me for? If I was connected with Vanderbilt or Astor I might set you up in business, but now I can't."

"Twenty-five cents will do," said Frank.

"Look here, Frank," said Dick, plunging his hands into his pocket, and drawing therefrom three pennies and a nickel, "do you see them?"

"Yes."

"Well, it's all the money I've got."

"I am afraid you have been extravagant, Dick," said Frank, in disappointment.

"Last night I went to Tony Pastor's, and when I got through I went into a saloon and got an ice cream and a cigar. You couldn't expect a feller to be very rich after that. I say, I'll lend you five cents if you want it."

"No, thank you, Dick. I'll wait till you are richer."

"I tell you what, Frank, I'll save up my money, and by day after to-morrow I guess I can set you up."

"Thank you, Dick. If I don't have the money by that time myself I'll accept your offer."

There was no other boy with whom Frank felt sufficiently well acquainted to request a loan, and he walked away, feeling rather disappointed. It was certainly provoking to think that nothing but the lack of a small sum stood between him and remunerative employment. Once started he determined not to spend quite all his earnings, but to improve upon his friend Dick's practice, and, if possible, get a little ahead.

When guiding the blind man he often walked up Broadway, and mechanically he took the same direction, walking slowly along, occasionally stopping to look in at a shop-window.

As he was sauntering along he found himself behind two gentlemen—one an old man, who wore gold spectacles; the other, a stout, pleasant-looking man, of middle age. Frank would not have noticed them particularly but for a sudden start and exclamation from the elder of the two gentlemen.

"I declare, Thompson," he said, "I've left my umbrella down-town."

"Where do you think you left it?"

"In Peckham's office; that is, I think I left it there."

"Oh, well, he'll save it for you."

"I don't know about that. Some visitor may carry it away."

"Never mind, Mr. Bowen. You are rich enough to afford a new one."

"It isn't the value of the article, Thompson," said his friend, in some emotion. "That umbrella was brought me from Paris by my son John, who died. It is as a souvenir of him that I regard and value it. I would not lose it for a hundred dollars, nay, five hundred."

"If you value it so much, sir, suppose we turn round and go back for it."

Frank had listened to this conversation, and an idea struck him. Pressing forward, he said respectfully, "Let me go for it, sir. I will get it, and bring it to your house."

The two gentlemen fixed their eyes upon the bright, eager face of the petitioner.

"Who are you, my boy?" asked Mr. Thompson.

"I am a poor boy, in want of work," answered our hero promptly.

"What is your name?"

"Frank Kavanagh."

"Where do you live?"

"I am trying to live in the city, sir."

"What have you been doing?"

"Leading a blind man, sir."

"Not a very pleasant employment, I should judge," said Thompson, shrugging his shoulders. "Well, have you lost that job?"

"Yes, sir."

"So the blind man turned you off, did he?"

"Yes, sir."

"Your services were unsatisfactory, I suppose?"

"He wanted me to pass counterfeit money for him, and I refused."

"If that is true, it is to your credit."

"It is true, sir," said Frank, quietly.

"Come, Mr. Bowen, what do you say—shall we accept this boy's services? It will save you time and trouble."

"If I were sure he could be trusted," said Bowen, hesitating. "He might pawn the umbrella. It is a valuable one."

"I hope, sir, you won't think so badly of me as that," said Frank, with feeling. "If I were willing to steal anything, it would not be a gift from your dead son."

"I'll trust you, my boy," said the old gentleman quickly. "Your tone convinces me that you may be relied upon."

"Thank you, sir."

The old gentleman drew a card from his pocket, containing his name and address, and on the reverse side wrote the name of the friend at whose office he felt sure the umbrella had been left, with a brief note directing that it be handed to the bearer.

"All right, sir."

"Stop a moment, my boy. Have you got money to ride?"

"No, sir."

"Here, take this, and go down at once in the next stage. The sooner you get there the better."

Frank followed directions. He stopped the next stage, and got on board. As he passed the City Hall Park, Dick Rafferty espied him. Frank nodded to him.

"How did he get money enough to ride in a 'bus?" Dick asked himself in much wonderment. "A few minutes ago he wanted to borrow some money of me, and now he's spending ten cents for a ride. Maybe he's found a pocket-book."

Frank kept on his way, and got out at Wall street. He found Mr. Peckham's office, and on presenting the card, much to his delight, the umbrella was handed him.

"Mr. Bowen was afraid to trust me with it over night," said Mr. Peckham, with a smile.

"He thought some visitor might carry it off," said Frank.

"Not unlikely. Umbrellas are considered common property."

Frank hailed another stage, and started on his way uptown. There was no elevated railway then, and this was the readiest conveyance, as Mr. Bowen lived on Madison avenue.

CHAPTER VII

AN INVITATION TO DINNER

" MR. BOWEN must be a rich man," thought Frank, as he paused on the steps of a fine brown-stone mansion, corresponding to the number on his card.

He rang the bell, and asked, " Is Mr. Bowen at home? "

" Yes, but he is in his chamber. I don't think he will see you."

" I think he will," said Frank, who thought the servant was taking too much upon herself, " as I come by his appointment."

" I suppose you can come into the hall," said the servant, reluctantly. " Is your business important? "

" You may tell him that the boy he sent for his umbrella has brought it. He was afraid he had lost it."

" He sets great store by that umbrella," said the girl, in a different tone. " I'll go and tell him."

Mr. Bowen came downstairs almost immediately. There was a look of extreme gratification upon his face.

" Bless my soul, how quick you were! " he exclaimed. " Why, I've only been home a few minutes. Did you find the umbrella at Mr. Peckham's office? "

" Yes, sir; it had been found, and taken care of."

" Did Peckham say anything? "

" He said you were probably afraid to trust it with him over night, but he smiled when he said it."

" Peckham will have his joke, but he is an excellent man. My boy, I am much indebted to you."

" I was very glad to do the errand, sir," said Frank.

" I think you said you were poor," said the old man, thoughtfully.

" Yes, sir. When I met you I hadn't a cent in the world."

"Haven't you any way to make a living?"

"Yes, sir. I could sell papers if I had enough money to set me up in business."

"Does it require a large capital?"

"Oh, no, sir," said Frank, smiling, "unless you consider fifty cents a large sum."

"Fifty cents!" repeated the old gentleman, in surprise. "You don't mean to say that this small sum would set you up in business?"

"Yes, sir; I could buy a small stock of papers, and buy more with what I received for them."

"To be sure. I didn't think of that."

Mr. Bowen was not a man of business. He had an ample income, and his tastes were literary and artistic. He knew more of books than of men, and more of his study than of the world.

"Well, my boy," he said after a pause, "how much do I owe you for doing this errand?"

"I leave that to you, sir. Whatever you think right will satisfy me."

"Let me see, you want fifty cents to buy papers, and you will require something to pay for your bed."

"Fifty cents in all will be enough, sir."

"I think I had better give you a dollar," said the old gentleman, opening his pocket-book.

Frank's eyes sparkled. A dollar would do him a great deal of good; with a dollar he would feel quite independent.

"Thank you, sir," he said. "It is more than I earned, but it will be very acceptable."

He put on his hat, and was about to leave the house, when Mr. Bowen suddenly said, "Oh, I think you'd better stay to dinner. It will be on the table directly. My niece is away, and if you don't stay I shall be alone."

Frank did not know what to say. He was rather abashed by the invitation, but, as the old gentleman was to be alone, it did not seem so formidable.

"I am afraid I don't look fit," he said.

"You can go upstairs and wash your face and hands. You'll find a clothes-brush there also. I'll ring for Susan to show you the way."

He rang the bell, and the girl who had admitted Frank made her appearance.

"Susan," said her master, "you may show this young gentleman into the back chamber on the third floor, and see that he is supplied with towels and all he needs. And you may lay an extra plate; he will dine with me."

Susan stared first at Mr. Bowen, and then at Frank, but did not venture to make any remark.

"This way, young man," she said, and ascended the front stairs, Frank following her closely.

She led the way into a handsomely furnished chamber, ejaculating, "Well, I never!"

"I hope you'll find things to your satisfaction, sir," she said, dryly. "If we'd known you were coming, we'd have made particular preparations for you."

"Oh, I think this will do," said Frank, smiling, for he thought it a good joke.

"I am glad you think it'll do," continued Susan. "Things mayn't be as nice as you're accustomed to at home."

"Not quite," said Frank, good-humoredly; "but I shan't complain."

"That's very kind and considerate of you, I'm sure," said Susan, tossing her head. "Well, I never did!"

"Nor I either, Susan," said Frank, laughing. "I am a poor boy, and I am not used to this way of living; so if you'll be kind enough to give me any hints, so I may behave properly at the table, I'll be very much obliged to you."

This frank acknowledgment quite appeased Susan, and she readily complied with our hero's request.

"But I must be going downstairs, or dinner will be

be late," she said, hurriedly. "You can come down when you hear the bell ring."

Frank had been well brought up, though not in the city, and he was aware that perfect neatness was one of the first characteristics of a gentleman. He therefore scrubbed his face and hands till they fairy shone, and brushed his clothes with great care. Even then they certainly did look rather shabby, and there was a small hole in the elbow of his coat; but, on the whole, he looked quite passable when he entered the dining-room.

"Take that seat, my boy," said his host.

Frank sat down and tried to look as if he was used to it.

"Take this soup to Mr. Kavanagh," said Mr. Bowen, in a dignified tone.

Frank started and smiled slightly, feeling more and more that it was an excellent joke.

"I wonder what Dick Rafferty would say if he could see me now," passed through his mind.

He acquitted himself very creditably, however, and certainly displayed an excellent appetite, much to the satisfaction of his hospitable host.

After dinner was over, Mr. Bowen detained him and began to talk of his dead son, telling anecdotes of his boyhood, to which Frank listened with respectful attention, for the father's devotion was touching.

"I think my boy looked a little like you," said the old gentleman. "What do you think, Susan?"

"Not a mite, sir," answered Susan, promptly.

"When he was a boy, I mean."

"I didn't know him when he was a boy, Mr. Bowen."

"No, to be sure not."

"But Mr. John was dark-complected, and this boy is light, and Mr. John's hair was black, and his is brown."

"I suppose I am mistaken," sighed the old man; "but there was something in the boy's face that reminded me of John."

"A little more, and he'll want to adopt him," thought Susan. "That wouldn't do nohow, though he does really seem like a decent sort of a boy."

At eight o'clock Frank rose, and wished Mr. Bowen good-night.

"Come and see me again, my boy," said the old gentleman, kindly. "You have been a good deal of company for me to-night."

"I am glad of it, sir."

"I think you might find something better to do than selling papers."

"I wish I could, sir."

"Come and dine with me again this day week, and I may have something to tell you."

"Thank you, sir."

Feeling in his pocket to see that his dollar was safe, Frank set out to walk down-town, repairing to the lodging-house, where he met Dick, and astonished that young man by the recital of his adventures.

"It takes you to get round, Frank," he said. "I wonder I don't get invited to dine on Madison avenue."

"I give it up," said Frank.

CHAPTER VIII

A NEWSBOY'S EXPERIENCES

FRANK slept that night at the lodging-house, and found a much better bed that he had been provided with by his late employer. He was up bright and early the next morning, and purchased a stock of morning papers. These he succeeded in selling during the forenoon, netting a profit of thirty cents. It was not much, but he was satisfied. At any rate he was a good deal better off than when in the employ of Mr. Mills. Of course he had to economize strictly, but the excellent arrangements of the lodging-house helped him to do this. Twelve cents provided him with lodging and breakfast. At noon, in company with his friend Dick, he went to a cheap restaurant, then to be found in Ann street, near Park row, and for fifteen cents enjoyed a dinner of two courses. The first consisted of a plate of beef, with a potato and a wedge of bread, costing ten cents, and the second, a piece of apple-pie.

"That's a good square meal," said Dick, in a tone of satisfaction. "I oughter get one every day, but sometimes I don't have the money."

"I should think you could raise fifteen cents a day for that purpose, Dick."

"Well, so I could; but then you see I save my money sometimes to go to the Old Bowery, or Tony Pastor's, in the evenin'."

"I would like to go, too, but I wouldn't give up my dinner. A boy that's growing needs enough to eat."

"I guess you're right," said Dick. "We'll go to dinner together every day, if you say so."

"All right, Dick; I should like your company."

About two o'clock in the afternoon, as Frank was resting on a bench in the City Hall Park, a girl of ten approached him. Frank recognized her as an inmate of the tenement-house where Mills, his late employer, lived.

"Do you want to see me?" asked Frank, observing that she was looking toward him.

"You're the boy that went round with the blind man, ain't you?" she asked.

"Yes."

"He wants you to come back."

Frank was rather surprised, but concluded that Mills had difficulty in obtaining a boy to succeed him. This was not very remarkable, considering the niggardly pay attached to the office.

" Did he send you to find me ? " asked our hero.

" Yes ; he says you needn't pass that money if you'll come back."

" Tell him that I don't want to come back," said Frank, promptly. " I can do better working for myself."

" He wants to know what you are doing," continued the girl.

" Does he? You can tell him that I am a newsboy."

" He says if you don't come back he'll have you arrested for stealing money from him. You mustn't be mad with me. That's what he told me to say."

" I don't blame you," said Frank, hotly ; " but you can tell him that he is a liar."

" Oh, I wouldn't dare to tell him that ; he would beat me."

" How can he do that, when he can't see where you are ? "

" I don't know how it is, but he can go right up to where you are just as well as if he could see."

" So he can. He's a humbug and a fraud. His eyes may not be very good, but he can see for all that. He pretends to be blind so as to make money."

" That's what mother and I think," said the girl. " So you won't come back ? "

" Not much. He can hire some other boy, and starve him. He won't get me."

" Ain't you afraid he'll have you arrested for stealing ? " asked the girl.

" If he tries that I'll expose him for wanting me to pass a counterfeit note. I never took a cent from him."

" He'll be awful mad," said the little girl.

" Let him. If he had treated me decently I would have stayed with him. Now I'm glad I left him."

Mills was indeed furious when, by degrees, he had drawn from his young messenger what Frank had said. He was sorry to lose him, for he was the most truthful and satisfactory guide he had ever employed, and he now regretted that he had driven him away by his unreasonable exactions. He considered whether it would be worth while to have Frank arrested on a false charge of theft, but was restrained by the fear that he would himself be implicated in passing counterfeit money, that is, in intention. He succeeded in engaging another boy, who really stole from him, and finally secured a girl, for whose services, however, he was obliged to pay her mother twenty cents every time she went out with him. Mean and miserly as he was, he agreed to this with reluctance, and only as a measure of necessity.

As he became more accustomed to his new occupation Frank succeeded better. He was a boy of considerable energy, and was on the alert for customers. It was not long before his earnings exceeded those of Dick Rafferty, who was inclined to take things easily.

One evening Dick was lamenting that he could not go to the Old Bowery.

" There's a bully play, Frank," he said. " There's a lot of fightin' in it."

" What is it called, Dick? "

" ' The Scalpers of the Plains.' There's five men murdered in the first act. Oh, it's elegant! "

" Why don't you go, then, Dick? "

" 'Cause I'm dead-broke—busted. That's why. I ain't had much luck this week, and it took all my money to pay for my lodgin's and grub."

" Do you want very much to go to the theater, Dick? "

" Of course I do; but it ain't no use. My credit ain't good, and I haven't no money in the bank."

" How much does it cost? "

" Fifteen cents, in the top gallery."

" Can you see there? "

" Yes, it's rather high up; but a feller with good eyes can see all he wants to there."

"I'll tell you what I'll do, Dick. You have been a good friend to me, and I'll take you at my expense."

"You will? To-night?"

"Yes."

"You're a reg'lar trump. We'll have a stavin' time. Sometime, when I'm flush, I'll return the compliment."

So the two boys went. They were at the doors early, and secured a front seat in the gallery. The performance was well adapted to please the taste of a boy, and they enjoyed it exceedingly. Dick was uproarious in his applause whenever a man was killed.

"Seems to me you like to see men killed, Dick," said his friend.

"Yes, it's kinder excitin'."

"I don't like that part so well as some others," said Frank.

"It's a stavin' play, ain't it?" asked Dick, greatly delighted.

Frank assented.

"I'll tell you what, Frank," said Dick; "I'd like to be a hunter and roam round the plains, killin' bears and Injuns."

"Suppose they should kill you? That wouldn't suit you so well, would it?"

"No, I guess not. But I'd like to be a hunter, wouldn't you?"

"No, I would rather live in New York. I would like to make a journey to the West if I had money enough; but I would leave the hunting to other men."

Dick, however, did not agree with his more sensible companion. Many boys like him are charmed with the idea of a wild life in the forest, and some have been foolish enough to leave good homes, and, providing themselves with what they considered necessary, have set out on a journey in quest of the romantic adventures which in stories had fired their imaginations. If their wishes could be realized it would not be long before the romance would fade out, and they would long for the good homes, which they had never before fully appreciated.

When the week was over, Frank found that he had lived within his means, as he had resolved to do; but he had not done much more. He began with a dollar which he had received from Mr. Bowen, and now he had a dollar and a quarter. There was a gain of twenty-five cents. There would have been a little more if he had not gone to the theater with Dick; but this he did not regret. He felt that he needed some amusement, and he wished to show his gratitude to his friend for various kind services. The time had come to accept Mr. Bowen's second dinner invitation. As Frank looked at his shabby clothes he wished there were a good pretext for declining, but he reflected that this would not be polite, and that the old gentleman would make allowances for his wardrobe. He brushed up his clothes as well as he could, and obtained a " *boss shine* " from Dick. Then he started for the house on Madison avenue.

" I'll lend you my clo'es if you want 'em," said Dick.

" There are too many spots of blacking on them, Dick. As I'm a newsboy, it wouldn't look appropriate. I shall have to make mine answer."

" I'll shine up the blackin' spots if you want me too."

" Never mind, Dick. I'll wait till next time for your suit."

CHAPTER IX

VICTOR DUPONT

As Frank was walking on Madison avenue, a little before reaching the house of Mr. Bowen he met a boy of his own age, whom he recognized. Victor Dupont had spent the previous summer at the hotel in the country village where Frank had lived until he came to the city. Victor

was proud of his social position, but time hung so heavily
upon his hands in the country that he was glad to keep
company with the village boys. Frank and he had frequently gone fishing together, and had been associated in
other amusements, so that they were for the time quite
intimate. The memories of home and past pleasures
thronged upon our hero as he met Victor, and his face
flushed with pleasure.

"Why, Victor," he said, eagerly, extending his hand,
"how glad I am to see you!"

Frank forgot that intimacy in the country does not
necessarily lead to intimacy in the city, and he was considerably surprised when Victor, not appearing to notice
his offered hand, said coldly, "I don't think I remember
you."

"Don't remember me!" exclaimed Frank, amazed.
"Why, I am Frank Kavanagh! Don't you remember how
much we were together last summer, and what good times
we had fishing and swimming together?"

"Yes, I believe I do remember you now," drawled Victor, still not offering his hand, or expressing any pleasure
at the meeting. "When did you come to the city?"

"I have been here two or three weeks," replied Frank.

"Oh, indeed! Are you going to remain?"

"Yes, if I can earn a living."

Victor scanned Frank's clothes with a critical, and evidently rather contemptuous, glance.

"What are you doing?" he asked. "Are you in a
store?"

"No; I am selling papers."

"A newsboy!" said Victor, with a curve of the lip.

"Yes," answered Frank, his pleasure quite chilled by
Victor's manner.

"Are you doing well?" asked Victor, more from curiosity than interest.

"I am making my expenses."

4 cc   4

"How do you happen to be in this neighborhood? I suppose you sell papers down-town."

"Yes, but I am invited to dinner."

"Not here—on the avenue!" ejaculated Victor.

"Yes," answered Frank, enjoying the other's surprise.

"Where?"

Frank mentioned the number.

"Why, that is next to my house. Mr. Bowen lives there."

"Yes."

"Perhaps you know some of the servants," suggested Victor.

"I know one," said Frank, smiling, for he read Victor's thoughts; "but my invitation comes from Mr. Bowen."

"Did you ever dine there before?" asked Victor, puzzled.

"Yes, last week."

"You must excuse my mentioning it, but I should hardly think you would like to sit down at a gentleman's table in that shabby suit."

"I don't," answered Frank; "but I have no better."

"Then you ought to decline the invitation."

"I would, but for appearing impolite."

"It seems very strange that Mr. Bowen should invite a newsboy to dinner."

"Perhaps if you'd mention what you think of it," said Frank, somewhat nettled, "he would recall the invitation."

"Oh, it's nothing to me," said Victor; "but I thought I'd mention it, as I know more of etiquette than you do."

"You are very considerate," said Frank, with a slight tinge of sarcasm in his tone.

By this time he had reached the house of Mr. Bowen, and the two boys parted.

Frank could not help thinking a little about what Victor had said. His suit, as he looked down at it, seemed shabbier than ever. Again it occurred to him that perhaps Mr. Bowen had forgotten the invitation, and this would make it very awkward for him. As he waited for the door to open he decided that, if it should appear that he was not expected, he would give some excuse, and go away.

Susan opened the door.

"Mr. Bowen invited me to come here to dinner to-night," began Frank, rather nervously.

"Yes, you are expected," said Susan, very much to his relief. "Wipe your feet, and come right in."

Frank obeyed.

"You are to go upstairs and get ready for dinner," said Susan, and she led the way to the same chamber into which our hero had been ushered the week before.

"There won't be much getting ready," thought Frank. "However, I can stay there till I hear the bell ring."

As he entered the room he saw a suit of clothes and some underclothing lying on the bed.

"They are for you," said Susan, laconically.

"For me!" exclaimed Frank, in surprise.

"Yes, put them on, and when you come down to dinner Mr. Bowen will see how they fit."

"Is it a present from him?" asked Frank, overwhelmed with surprise and gratitude, for he could see that the clothes were very handsome.

"Well, they ain't from me," said Susan, "so it's likely they come from him. Don't be too long, for Mr. Bowen doesn't like to have any one late to dinner."

Susan had been in the service of her present mistress fifteen years, and was a privileged character. She liked to have her own way; but had sterling qualities, being neat, faithful, and industrious.

"I wonder whether I am awake or dreaming," thought Frank, when he was left alone. "I shouldn't like to wake up and find it was all a dream."

He began at once to change his shabby clothes for the

new ones. He found that the articles provided were a complete outfit, including shirt, collar, cuffs, stockings; in fact, everything that was needful. The coat, pants, and vest were a neat gray, and proved to be an excellent fit. In the bosom of the shirt were neat studs, and the cuffs were supplied with sleeve-buttons to correspond. When Frank stood before the glass, completely attired, he hardly knew himself. He was as well dressed as his aristocratic acquaintance, Victor Dupont, and looked more like a city boy than a boy bred in the country.

"I never looked so well in my life," thought our young hero, complacently. "How kind Mr. Bowen is!"

Frank did not know it; but he was indebted for this gift to Susan's suggestion. When her master told her in the morning that Frank was coming to dinner, she said, "It's a pity the boy hasn't some better clothes."

"I didn't notice his clothes," said Mr. Bowen. "Are they shabby?"

"Yes; and they are almost worn out. They don't look fit for one who is going to sit at your table."

"Bless my soul! I never thought of that. You think he needs some new clothes."

"He needs them badly."

"I will call at Baldwin's, and order some ready-made; but I don't know his size."

"He's about two inches shorter than you, Mr. Bowen. Tell 'em that, and they will know. He ought to have shirts and stockings, too."

"So he shall," said the old man, quite interested. "He shall have a full rig-out from top to toe. Where shall I go for the shirts and things?"

Susan had a nephew about Frank's age, and she was prepared to give the necessary information. The old gentleman, who had no business to attend to, was delighted to have something to fill up his time. He went out directly after breakfast, or as soon as he had read the morning paper, and made choice of the articles already described, giving strict injunctions that they should be sent home immediately.

This was the way Frank got his new outfit.

When our hero came downstairs Mr. Bowen was waiting eagerly to see the transformation. The result delighted him.

"Why, I shouldn't have known you!" he exclaimed, lifting both hands. "I had no idea new clothes would change you so much."

"I don't know how to thank you, sir," said Frank, gratefully.

"I never should have thought of it if it hadn't been for Susan."

"Then I thank you, Susan," said Frank, offering his hand to the girl, as she entered the room.

Susan was pleased. She liked to be appreciated; and she noted with satisfaction the great improvement in Frank's appearance.

"You are quite welcome," she said; "but it was master's money that paid for the clothes."

"It was your kindness that made him think of it," said Frank.

From that moment Susan became Frank's fast friend. We generally like those whom we have benefited, if our services are suitably acknowledged.

CHAPTER X

A NEW PROSPECT

"Well, Frank, and how is your business?" asked the old gentleman, when they were sitting at the dinner-table.

"Pretty good, sir."

"Are you making your expenses?"

"Yes, sir; just about."

"That is well. Mind you never run into debt. That is a bad plan."

"I shan't have to now, sir. If I had had to buy clothes for myself, I might have had to."

"Do you find the shirts and stockings fit you?"

"Yes, sir; they are just right."

"I bought half a dozen of each. Susan will give you the bundle when you are ready to go. If they had not been right, they could have been exchanged."

"Thank you, sir. I shall feel rich with so many clothes."

"Where do you sleep, Frank?"

"At the Newsboys' Lodging-House."

"Is there any place there where you can keep your clothes?"

"Yes, sir. Each boy has a locker to himself."

"That is a good plan. It would be better if you had a room to yourself."

"I can't afford it yet, sir. The lodging-house costs me only forty-two cents a week for a bed, and I could not get a room for that."

"Bless my soul! That is very cheap. Really, I think I could save money by giving up my house, and going there to sleep."

"I don't think you would like it, sir," said Frank, smiling.

"Probably not. Now, Frank, I am going to mention a plan I have for you. You don't want to be a newsboy all your life."

"No, sir; I think I should get tired of it by the time I was fifty."

"My friend Thompson, the gentleman who was walking with me when we first saw you, is an officer of the American District Telegraph Company. They employ a large number of boys at their various offices to run errands; and, in fact, to do anything that is required of them. Probably you have seen some of the boys going about the city."

" Yes, sir ; they have a blue uniform."

" Precisely. How would you like to get a situation of that kind? "

" Very much, sir," said Frank, promptly.

" Would you like it better than being a newsboy? "

" Yes, sir."

" My friend Thompson, to whom I spoke on the subject, says he will take you on in a few weeks, provided you will qualify yourself for the post."

" I will do that, sir, if you will tell me how."

" You must be well acquainted with the city in all its parts, know the locations of different hotels, prominent buildings, have a fair education, and be willing to make yourself generally useful. You will have to satisfy the superintendent that you are fitted for the position."

" I think my education will be sufficient," said Frank, " for I always went to school till just before I came to the city. I know something about the lower part of the city, but I will go about every day during the hours when I am not selling papers till I am familiar with all parts of it."

" Do so, and when there is a vacancy I will let you know."

" How much pay shall I get, sir, if they accept me? "

" About three dollars a week at first, and more when you get familiar with your duties. No doubt money will also be given you by some who employ you, though you will not be allowed to ask for any fees. Very likely you will get nearly as much in this way as from your salary."

Frank's face expressed satisfaction.

" That will be bully," he said.

" I beg pardon," said the old gentleman, politely. " What did you remark? "

" That will be excellent," said Frank, blushing.

"I thought you spoke of a bully."

"It was a word I learned from Dick Rafferty," said Frank, feeling rather embarrassed.

"And who is Dick Rafferty?"

"One of my friends at the Lodging-House."

"Unless his education is better than yours I would not advise you to learn any of his words."

"I beg your pardon, sir."

"You must excuse my offering you advice. It is the privilege of the old to advise the young."

"I shall always be glad to follow your advice, Mr. Bowen," said Frank.

"Good boy, good boy," said the old gentleman, approvingly. "I wish all boys were like you. Some think they know more than their grandfathers. There's one of that kind who lives next door."

"His name is Victor Dupont, isn't it, sir?"

Mr. Bowen looked surprised. "How is it that you know his name?" he asked.

"We were together a good deal last summer. His family boarded at the hotel in the country village where I used to live. He and I went bathing and fishing together."

"Indeed! Have you seen him since you came to the city?"

"I met him as I was on my way here this afternoon."

"Did he speak to you?"

"Yes, sir; though at first he pretended he didn't remember me."

"Just like him. He is a very proud and conceited boy. Did you tell him you were coming to dine with me?"

"Yes, sir. He seemed very much surprised, as I had just told him I was a newsboy. He said he was surprised that you should invite a newsboy to dine with you."

"I would much rather have you dine with me than him. What more did he say?"

"He said he shouldn't think I would like to go out to dinner with such a shabby suit."

"We have removed that objection," said Mr. Bowen, smiling.

"Yes, sir," said Frank; "I think Victor will treat me more respectfully now when he meets me."

"The respect of such a boy is of very little importance. He judges only by the outside."

At an early hour Frank took his leave, promising to call again before long.

"Where can I send to you if you are wanted for a telegraph boy?" asked Mr. Bowen.

"A letter to me addressed to the care of Mr. O'Connor at the lodging-house will reach me," said Frank.

"Write it down for me," said the old gentleman. "You will find writing materials on yonder desk."

When Frank made his appearance at the lodging-house in his new suit, with two bundles, one containing his old clothes, and the other his extra supply of underclothing, his arrival made quite a sensation.

"Have you come into a fortun'?" asked one boy.

"Did you draw a prize in the Havana lottery?" asked another.

"Have you been playing policy?" asked a third.

"You're all wrong," said Dick Rafferty. "Frank's been adopted by a rich man upon Madison avenue. Ain't that so, Frank?"

"Something like it," said Frank. "There's a gentleman up there who has been very kind to me."

"If he wants to adopt another chap, spake a good word for me," said Patsy Reagan.

"Whisht, Patsy, he don't want no Irish bog-trotter," said Phil Donovan.

"You're Irish yourself, Phil, now, and you can't deny it."

"What if I am? I ain't no bog-trotter—I'm the son

of an Irish count. You can see by my looks that I belong
to the gintry."

" Then the gintry must have red hair and freckles,
Phil. There ain't no chance for you."

" Tell us all about it, Frank," said Dick. " Shure I'm
your best friend, and you might mention my name to the
ould gintleman if he's got any more good clothes to give
away."

" I will with pleasure, Dick, if I think it will do any
good."

" You won't put on no airs because you're better dressed
than the likes of us? "

" I shall wear my old clothes to-morrow, Dick. I can't
afford to wear my best clothes every day."

" I can," said Dick, dryly, which was quite true, as
his best clothes were the only ones he had.

Bright and early the next morning Frank was about
his work, without betraying in any way the proud consciousness of being the owner of two suits. He followed
Mr. Bowen's advice, and spent his leisure hours in explor-
ing the city in its various parts, so that in the course of a
month he knew more about it than boys who had lived
in it all their lives. He told Dick his object in taking
these long walks, and urged him to join him in the hope
of winning a similar position; but Dick decided that it
was too hard work. He preferred to spend his leisure
time in playing marbles or pitching pennies.

CHAPTER XI

THE TELEGRAPH BOY

Six weeks later Frank Kavanagh, through the influence of his patron, found himself in the uniform of a District Telegraph Messenger. The blue suit, and badge
upon the cap, are familiar to every city resident. The uni-

form is provided by the company, but must be paid for by weekly instalments, which are deducted from the wages of the wearers. This would have seriously embarrassed Frank but for an opportune gift of ten dollars from Mr. Bowen, which nearly paid the expense of his suit.

Frank was employed in one of the up-town offices of the company. For the information of such of my young readers as live in the country it may be explained that large numbers of houses and offices in the city are connected with the offices of the District Telegraph by machines, through which, at any time in the day or night, a messenger may be summoned for any purpose. It is only necessary to raise a knob in the box provided, and a bell is rung in the office of the company. Of course there is more or less transient business besides that of the regular subscribers.

Boys, on arriving at the office, seat themselves, and are called upon in order. A boy just returned from an errand hangs up his hat, and takes his place at the foot of the line. He will not be called upon again till all who are ahead of him have been dispatched in one direction or another.

Frank was curious to know what would be his first duty, and waited eagerly for his turn to come.

At length it came.

"Go to No. — Madison avenue," said the superinténdent.

A few minutes later Frank was ascending the steps of a handsome brown-stone residence.

"Oh, you're the telegraph boy," said a colored servant. You're to go upstairs into missus's sitting-room."

Upon entering, Frank found himself in the presence of a rather stout lady, who was reclining on a sofa.

He bowed politely, and waited for his instructions.

"I hope you are a trustworthy boy," said the stout lady.

"I hope so, ma'am."

"Come here, Fido," said the lady.

A little mass of hair, with two red eyes peeping out, rose from the carpet and waddled toward the lady, for Fido was about as stout as his mistress.

"Do you like dogs?" asked Mrs. Leroy, for this was the lady's name.

"Yes, ma'am," answered Frank, wondering what that had to do with his errand.

"I sent for you to take my sweet darling out for an airing. His health requires that he should go out every day. I generally take him myself, but this morning I have a severe headache, and do not feel equal to the task. My dear little pet, will you go out with this nice boy?"

Fido looked gravely at Frank and sneezed.

"I hope the darling hasn't got cold," said Mrs. Leroy, with solicitude. "My lad, what is your name?"

"Frank Kavanagh, ma'am."

"Will you take great care of my little pet, Frank?"

"I will try to, madam. Where do you want him to go?"

"To Madison Park. He always likes the park, because it is so gay. When you get there you may sit down on one of the benches and give him time to rest."

"Yes, ma'am. How long would you like me to stay out with him?"

"About an hour and a half. Have you a watch?"

"No; but I can tell the time by the clock in front of the Fifth Avenue Hotel."

"To be sure. I was going to lend you my watch."

"Shall I start now?"

"Yes. Here is the string. Don't make Fido go too fast. He is stout, and cannot walk fast. You will be sure to take great care of him?"

"Yes, madam."

"And you keep watch that no bad man carries off my

Fido. I used to send him out by one of the girls, till I
found that she ill-treated the poor thing. Of course I
couldn't stand that, so I sent her packing, I can tell you."

"I will try to follow your directions," said Frank, who
wanted to laugh at the lady's ridiculous devotion to her
ugly little favorite.

"That is right. You look like a good boy. I will
give you something for yourself when you come back."

"Thank you, ma'am," said Frank, who was better
pleased with this remark than any the lady had previously
made.

Mrs. Leroy kissed Fido tenderly, and consigned him to
the care of our hero.

"I suppose," said Frank to himself, "that I am the
dog's nurse. It is rather a queer office; but as long as I
am well paid for it I don't mind."

When Fido found himself on the sidewalk he seemed
disinclined to move; but after a while, by dint of coax-
ing, he condescended to waddle along at Frank's heels.

After a while they reached Madison Park, and Frank,
according to his instructions, took a seat, allowing Fido
to curl up at his side.

"This isn't very hard work," thought Frank. "I wish
I had a book or paper to read, to while away the time."

While he was sitting there Victor Dupont came sauntering along.

"Halloa!" he exclaimed, in surprise, as he recognized
Frank, "is that you?"

"I believe it is," answered Frank, with a smile.

"Are you a telegraph boy?"

"Yes."

"I thought you were a newsboy?"

"So I was; but I have changed by business."

"What are you doing here?"

"Taking care of a dog," said Frank, laughing.

"Is that the dog?"

" Yes."

" It's a beastly little brute. What's its name? "

" Fido."

" Who does it belong to? "

Frank answered.

" I know," said Victor; " it's a fat lady living on the avenue. I have seen her out often with little pug. How do you feel, Fido? " and Victor began to pull the hair of the lady's favorite.

" Don't do that, Victor," remonstrated Frank.

" Why not? "

" Mrs. Leroy wouldn't like it."

" Mrs. Leroy isn't here."

" I am," said Frank, emphatically, " and that is the same thing."

Victor, by way of reply, pinched Fido's ear, and the little animal squeaked his disapproval.

" Look here, Victor," said Frank, decidedly, " you must stop that."

" Must I? " sneered Victor, contemptuously. " Suppose I don't? "

" Then I shall punch you," said Frank, quietly.

" You are impertinent," said Victor, haughtily. " You needn't put on such airs because you are nurse to a puppy."

" That is better than being a puppy myself," retorted Frank.

" Do you mean to insult me? " demanded Victor, quickly.

" No, unless you choose to think the remark fits you."

" I have a great mind to give you a thrashing," said Victor, furiously.

" Of course I should sit still and let you do it," said Frank, calmly. " Fido is under my care, and I can't have him teased. That is right, isn't it? "

" I did wrong to notice you," said Victor. " You are only a dog's nurse."

Frank laughed.

"You are right," he said. "It is new business for me, and though it is easy enough I can't say I like it. However, I am in the service of the Telegraph Company, and must do whatever is required."

Victor walked away, rather annoyed because he could not tease Frank.

"The boy has no pride," he said to himself, "or he wouldn't live out to take care of dogs. But, then, it is suitable enough for him."

"Is that dawg yours?" asked a rough-looking man, taking his seat on the bench near Frank.

"No, sir."

"How old is it?"

"I don't know."

"Looks like a dawg I used to own. Let me take him."

"I would rather not," said Frank, coldly. "It belongs to a lady who is very particular."

"Oh, you won't, won't you?" said the man, roughly. "Danged if I don't think it is my dawg, after all;" and the man seized Fido, and was about to carry him away.

But Frank seized him by the arm, and called for help.

"What's the matter?" asked a park policeman who, unobserved by either, had come up behind.

"This man is trying to steal my dog," said Frank.

"The dog is mine," said the thief, boldly.

"Drop him!" said the officer, authoritatively. "I have seen that dog before. He belongs to neither of you."

"That is true," said Frank. "It belongs to Mrs. Leroy, of Madison avenue, and I am employed to take it out for an airing."

"It's a lie!" said the man, sullenly.

"If you are seen again in this neighborhood," said the policeman, "I shall arrest you. Now clear out!"

The would-be thief slunk away, and Frank thanked the officer.

" That man is a dog-stealer," said the policeman. " His business is to steal dogs, and wait till a reward is offered. Look out for him! "

CHAPTER XII

A WAYWARD SON

WHEN Frank carried Fido back to his mistress he thought it his duty to tell Mrs. Leroy of the attempt to abduct the favorite.

Mrs. Leroy turned pale.

" Did the man actually take my little pet? " she asked.

" Yes, ma'am. He said it was his dog."

" The horrid brute! How could I have lived without my darling? " and the lady caressed her favorite tenderly. " How did you prevent him? "

" I seized him by the arm, and held him till a policeman came up."

" You are a brave boy," said Mrs. Leroy, admiringly. " But for you, Fido would have been stolen."

" The policeman said the man was a professional dog-stealer. He steals dogs for the reward which is offered."

" I was sure I could trust you with my pet," said Mrs. Leroy. " You deserve a reward yourself."

" I was only doing my duty, ma'am," said Frank, modestly.

" It isn't everybody that does that."

Mrs. Leroy rose, and, going to her bureau, drew an ivory portemonnaie from a small upper drawer; from this she extracted a two-dollar bill, and gave it to Frank.

" This is too much," said Frank, surprised at the size of the gift.

" Too much for rescuing my little pet? No, no, I am the best judge of that. I wouldn't have lost him for fifty times two dollars."

"You are very liberal, and I am very much obliged to you," said Frank.

"If I send again for a boy to take out Fido, I want you to come."

"I will if I can, ma'am."

For several days, though Frank was employed on errands daily, there was nothing of an unusual character. About eleven o'clock one evening (for Frank had to take his turn at night work) he was sent to a house on West Thirty-eighth street. On arriving, he was ushered into the presence of a lady of middle age, whose anxious face betrayed the anxiety that she felt.

"I have a son rather larger and older than you," she said, "who, to my great sorrow, has been led away by evil companions, who have induced him to drink and play cards for money. I will not admit them into my house, but I cannot keep him from seeking them out. He is no doubt with them to-night."

Frank listened with respectful sympathy, and waited to hear what he was desired to do in the matter.

"The boy's father is dead," continued Mrs. Vivian, with emotion, "and I cannot fill his place. Fred is unwilling to obey his mother. His companions have persuaded him that it is unmanly."

"I would gladly obey my mother if I could have her back," said Frank.

"Is your mother dead, then?" inquired Mrs. Vivian, with quick sympathy.

"I have neither father nor mother," Frank answered gravely.

"Poor boy! And yet you do not fall into temptation."

"I have no time for that, ma'am; I have to earn my living."

"If I could get Fred to take a position it might be a benefit to him," said Mrs. Vivian, thoughtfully. "But the question now is, how I may be able to find him."

5 cc   5

" When did you see him last? " asked Frank.

" About three o'clock this afternoon I gave him seventy-five dollars, and sent him to pay a bill. I was perhaps imprudent to trust him with such a sum of money; but for a few days past he has been more steady than usual, and I thought it would show my confidence in him if I employed him in such a matter."

" I should think it would, ma'am."

" But I am afraid Fred fell in with some of his evil companions, and let them know that he was well provided with money. That would be enough to excite their cupidity."

" Who are the companions you speak of? " asked Frank.

" Boys, or rather young men, for they are all older than Fred, of lower social rank than himself. I don't attach any special importance to that, nor do I object to them on that ground; but they are, I have reason to think, ill-bred and disreputable. They know Fred to be richer than themselves, and induce him to drink and play, in the hope of getting some of his money. I have sent for you to go in search of my son. If you find him you must do your best to bring him home."

" I will," said Frank. " Can you give me any idea where he may be found? "

Mrs. Vivian wrote on a card two place—one a billiard-saloon, which she had reason to suspect that her son frequented.

" Now," said Frank, " will you be kind enough to describe your son to me, so that I may know him when I see him? "

" I will show you his photograph," said Mrs. Vivian.

She opened an album, and showed the picture of a boy of seventeen, with a pleasant face, fair complexion, and hair somewhat curly. His forehead was high, and he looked gentlemanly and refined.

" Is he not good-looking? " said the mother.

"He looks like a gentleman," said Frank.

"He would be one if he could throw off his evil associates. Do you think you will know him from the picture?"

"Yes, I think so. Is he tall?"

"Two or three inches taller than you are. You had better take the picture with you. I have an extra one, which you can put in your pocket to help you identify him. By the way, it will be as well that you should be supplied with money in case it is necessary to bring him home in a cab."

Frank understood what the mother found it difficult to explain. She feared that her boy might be the worse for drink.

She handed our hero a five-dollar bill.

"I will use it prudently, madam," said he, "and account to you for all I do not use."

"I trust you wholly," said the lady. "Now go as quickly as possible."

Frank looked at the two addresses he had on the card. The billiard-saloon was on the east side of the city, in an unfashionable locality.

"I'll go there first," he decided.

Crossing to Third avenue he hailed a car, and rode down-town. His knowledge of the city, gained from the walks he took when a newsboy, made it easy for him to find the place of which he was in search. Though it was nearly midnight, the saloon was lighted up, and two tables were in use. On the left-hand side, as he entered, was a bar, behind which stood a man in his shirt-sleeves, who answered the frequent calls for drinks. He looked rather suspiciously at Frank's uniform when he entered.

"What do you want?" he asked. "Have you any message for me?"

"No," said Frank, carelessly. "Let me have a glass of lemonade."

The bar-keeper's face cleared instantly, and he set about preparing the beverage required.

"Won't you have something in it?" he asked.

"No, sir," said Frank.

"You boys are kept out pretty late," said the bar-keeper, socially.

"Not every night," said Frank. "We take turns."

Frank paid ten cents for his lemonade, and, passing into the billiard-saloon, sat down and watched a game. He looked around him, but could not see anything of Fred. In fact, all the players were men.

Sitting next to him was a young fellow, who was watching the game.

"Suppose we try a game," he said to Frank.

"Not to-night. I came in here to look for a friend, but I guess he isn't here."

"I've been here two hours. What does your friend look like?"

"That's his picture," said Frank, displaying the photograph.

"Oh, yes," said his new acquaintance, "he is here now. His name is Fred, isn't it?"

"Yes," answered Frank, eagerly; "I don't see him. Where is he?"

"He's playing cards upstairs, but I don't believe he can tell one card from the other."

"Been drinking, I suppose," said Frank, betraying no surprise.

"I should say so. Do you know the fellows he's with?"

"I am not sure about that. How long has Fred been upstairs?"

"About an hour. He was playing billiards till he couldn't stand straight, and then they went upstairs."

"Would you mind telling him that there is a friend downstairs who wishes to see him, that is, if you know the way?"

"Oh, yes, I live here. Won't you come up with me?"

"Perhaps I had better," said Frank, and followed his companion through a door in the rear, and up a dark and narrow staircase to the street floor.

"It'll be a hard job to get him away," thought Frank; "but, for his mother's sake, I will do my best."

CHAPTER XIII

A TIMELY RESCUE

As Frank entered the room he hastily took in the scene before him. Round a table sat three young men, of not far from twenty, the fourth side being occupied by Fred Vivian. They were playing cards, and sipping drinks as they played. Fred Vivian's handsome face was flushed, and he was nervously excited. His hands trembled as he lifted the glass, and his wandering, uncertain glances showed that he was not himself.

"It's your play, Fred," said his partner.

Fred picked up a card without looking at it, and threw it down on the table.

"That settles it," said another. "Fred, old boy, you've lost the game. You're another five dollars out."

Fred fumbled in his pocket for a bill, and it was quickly taken from his hand before he could well see of what value it was. Frank, however, quickly as it was put away, saw that it was a ten. It was clear that Fred was being cheated in the most barefaced manner.

Frank's entrance was evidently unwelcome to most of the company.

"What are you bringing in that boy for, John?" demanded a low-browed fellow, with a face like a bull-dog.

"He is a friend of Fred's," answered John.

"He's a telegraph boy. He comes here a spy. Fred don't know him. Clear out, boy!"

Frank took no notice of this hostile remark, but walked up to Fred Vivian.

"Fred," said he, thinking it best to speak as if he knew him, "it is getting late, and your mother is anxious about you. Won't you come home with me?"

"Who are you?" asked Fred, with drunken gravity. "You ain't my mother."

"I come from your mother. Don't you know me? I am Frank Kavanagh."

"How do, Frank? Glad to see you, ol' feller. Take a drink. Here, you boy, bring a drink for my frien', Frank Kavanagh."

The three others looked on disconcerted. They were not ready to part with Fred yet, having secured only a part of his money.

"You don't know him, Fred," said the one who had appropriated the ten-dollar bill. "He's only a telegraph boy."

"I tell you he's my frien', Frank Kav'nagh," persisted Fred, with an obstinacy not unusual in one in his condition.

"Well, if he is, let him sit down, and have a glass of something hot."

"No, I thank you," said Frank, coldly. "Fred and I are going home."

"No, you're not," exclaimed the other, bringing his fist heavily down upon the table. "We won't allow our friend Fred to be kidnapped by a boy of your size—not much we won't, will we, boys?"

"No! no!" chimed in the other two.

Fred Vivian looked at them undecided.

"I guess I'd better go," he stammered. "There's something the matter with my head."

"You need another drink to brace you up. Here, John, bring up another punch for Fred."

Frank saw that unless he got Fred away before drinking

any more, he would not be in a condition to go at all. It was a critical position, but he saw that he must be bold and resolute.

"You needn't bring Fred anything more," he said. "He has had enough already."

"I have had enough already," muttered Fred, mechanically.

"Boys, are we going to stand this?" said the low-browed young man. "Are we going to let this telegraph boy interfere with a social party of young gentlemen? I move that we throw him downstairs."

He half rose as he spoke, but Frank stood his ground.

"You'd better not try it," he said, quietly, "unless you want to pass the night in the station-house."

"What do you mean, you young jackanapes?" said the other angrily. "What charge can you trump up against us?"

"You have been cheating Fred out of his money," said Frank, firmly.

"It's a lie! We've been having a friendly game, and he lost. If we'd lost, we would have paid."

"How much did he lose?"

"Five dollars."

"And you took ten from him."

"It's a lie!" repeated the other; but he looked disconcerted.

"It is true, for I noticed the bill as you took it from him. But it's not much worse than playing for money with him when he is in no condition to understand the game. You'd better give him back that ten-dollar bill."

"I've a great mind to fling you downstairs, you young scamp!"

"You are strong enough to do it," said Frank, exhibiting no trace of fear, "but I think you would be sorry for it afterwards. Come, Fred."

Though Frank was so much younger and smaller, there was something in his calm, self-possessed manner that gave him an ascendency over the weak, vacillating Fred. The latter rose, and, taking our hero's arm, turned to leave the room.

"Let him go," said the leader, who had been made uneasy by Frank's threat, and saw that it was politic to postpone his further designs upon his intended victim. "If he chooses to obey a small telegraph boy, he can."

"Don't mind him, Fred," said Frank. "You know I'm your friend."

"My friend, Frank Kavanagh!" repeated Fred, drowsily. "I'm awful sleepy, Frank. I want to go to bed."

"You shall go to bed as soon as you get home, Fred."

"I say, boy," said the leader, uneasily, "that was all a lie about the ten-dollar bill. You didn't see straight. Did he, Bates?"

"Of course he didn't."

"One lies and the other swears to it," thought Frank.

"Nothing will be done about it," he said, "if you will let Fred alone hereafter. The money you have won from him belongs to his mother, and, unless you keep away from him, she will order your arrest."

"You're altogether too smart for a boy of your size," sneered the other. "Take your friend away. We don't care to associate with a milksop, who allows himself to be ordered around by women and children."

Fortunately Fred was too drowsy to pay heed to what was being said; in fact, he was very sleepy, and was anxious to go to bed. Frank got him into a cab, and in twenty minutes they safely reached his mother's house in Thirty-eighth street.

Mrs. Vivian was anxiously awaiting the return of the prodigal.

"O Fred," she said, "how could you stay away so,

when you know how worried I get? You have been drinking, too."

"This is my friend, Frank Kavanagh," hiccoughed Fred.

"Shall I go up and help put him to bed?" asked Frank.

"Does he require help?" asked Mrs. Vivian, sorrowfully.

"He has been drinking a good deal."

"Yes, you may go up. I will lead the way to his chamber. Afterwards I want to speak to you."

"All right."

"Where did you find him?" asked Mrs. Vivian, when Frank with some difficulty had prepared his charge for bed.

"In the billiard-saloon to which you directed me. He was upstairs playing cards for money. They were cheating him in the most outrageous manner."

"I suppose they got all his money."

"Not all; but they would soon have done so. Here is his pocket-book, which I just took from his pocket."

"There are twenty dollars left," said Mrs. Vivian, after an examination. "They must have secured the rest. O my poor boy! Would that I could shield you from these dangerous companions!"

"I don't think they will trouble him again, Mrs. Vivian."

"Why not? You do not know them."

"I told them that, if they came near him, hereafter, you would have them arrested for swindling your son out of money belonging to you."

"Will that have any effect upon them?"

"Yes, because they know that I am ready to appear as a witness against them."

"Did Fred show any unwillingness to come with you?"

"No; I made him think I was an old acquaintance of his. Besides, he was feeling sleepy."

"You have acted with great judgment for so young a lad," said Mrs. Vivian. "I wish Fred had a companion like you to influence him for good. Where do you live?"

"At the Newsboys' Lodging-House. I cannot afford to hire a room."

Mrs. Vivian looked thoughtful.

"Give me your name and address," she said.

These she noted down.

"I won't keep you any longer to-night," she said, "for you must be tired. You will hear from me again."

"Oh," said Frank, "I nearly forgot. Here is the balance of the money you handed me for expenses."

"Keep it for yourself," said Mrs. Vivian, "and accept my thanks besides."

Though Frank had paid for the cab, there was a balance of nearly two dollars in his hands which he was very glad to keep.

CHAPTER XIV

FRANK MAKES AN EVENING CALL

THE next day Frank chanced to meet Mrs. Vivian in the street. She recognized him at once.

"I see you are kept busy," she said, pleasantly.

"Yes," answered Frank. "Our business is pretty good just now. How is your son?"

"He slept well, and woke much refreshed this morning. He is a good boy naturally, but unable to withstand temptation. I have decided to send him to the country for a few weeks, to visit a cousin of about his own age. There he will be secure from temptation, and will have a chance to ride. I would have sent him away before, but that it would leave me alone in the house. You told me last evening that you had no boarding-place."

"My only home is at the lodging-house," said Frank.

"How would you like to occupy a room at my house while my son is away?"

"Very much," said Frank, promptly.

"I shall find it convenient to have you in the house, and shall feel safer."

"I am afraid I shouldn't be a match for an able-bodied burglar," said Frank, smiling.

"Perhaps not; but you could summon a policeman. When can you come and see me about this arrangement?"

"I am off duty to-night."

"Very well; I will expect you. Fred will not go away till to-morrow, and you will have a chance to see him under more favorable circumstances than last evening."

"Thank you very much for your kind invitation," said Frank, politely.

Mrs. Vivian bade him good-morning, very favorably impressed with his manners and deportment.

Frank looked upon the proposal made him by Mrs. Vivian as a piece of great good-fortune. In his new position, excellent as were the beds at the lodging-house, he found it inconvenient to go there to sleep Once or twice, on account of the late hour at which he was released from duty, he was unable to secure admittance, and had to pay fifty cents for a bed at a hotel on the European system. He had for some time been thinking seriously of hiring a room; but the probable expense deterred him. At Mrs. Vivian's he would have nothing to pay.

In the evening he changed his uniform for the neat suit given him by Mr. Bowen, and about eight o'clock rang the bell of the house in Thirty-eighth street.

He was at once ushered into the presence of Mrs. Vivian and her son.

"I am glad to see you, my young friend," said Mrs. Vivian, glancing with approval at the neat appearance of her young visitor. "Fred, this is the young man who brought you home last night."

"I am much obliged to you," said Fred Vivian, offering his hand to Frank. "I am ashamed of having been found in such a place."

"I don't think the young men with you were very much your friends," said Frank; "I detected one in cheating you."

"You mean at cards?"

"I don't mean that, though I presume they did; but you handed a ten-dollar bill to one of them, and he took it as a five."

"Are you sure of that?" asked Fred, his face flushing with indignation.

"Yes, I saw the number of the bill, though he put it away very quickly."

"And I had been treating that fellow all the afternoon! I gave him a good dinner, too."

"Are you surprised at such treatment from such a person?" asked his mother. "I should have expected it."

"I will never notice the fellow again as long as I live," said Fred, who seemed a good deal impressed by his companion's treachery. "Why, it's nothing better than robbery."

"You have given it the right name, Fred," said his mother, quietly.

"He ought to give the money back," said Fred.

"Let it go, my son. I am willing to lose it, if it severs all acquaintance between you and your unworthy companion."

"Have I ever met you before?" asked Fred, turning to Frank.

"Not before last evening."

"I thought you spoke of yourself as an old acquaintance."

"That was to induce you to come with me," explained Frank. "I hope you will excuse the deception."

"Certainly I will. I had been drinking so much that it was quite necessary to treat me as a child; but I don't mean to be caught in such a scrape again."

"May you keep that resolution, Fred!" said his mother, earnestly.

"I will try to, mother."

"My mother tells me that you are going to take my place while I am in the country," said Fred, turning to Frank.

"I shall be very glad to do so," said our hero. "I never had such a good home before."

"You are a telegraph boy, are you not?" asked Fred.

"Yes," answered Frank.

"Tell me about it. Is it hard work?"

"Not hard, but sometimes when I have been kept pretty busy, I get tired toward night."

"I should think it would be rather good fun," said Fred.

"Do you think you would like it?" asked his mother, with a smile.

"I might like it for about half a day, but all day would be too much for me. However, I am too old for such a position."

Fred had no false pride, and though he knew that Frank was in a social position considerably below his own, he treated him as an equal. Those who are secure of their own position are much more likely to avoid "putting on airs" than those who have recently been elevated in the social scale. Frank was destined that same evening to see the contrast between true and false gentility.

It so happened that Victor Dupont, already mentioned, was an acquaintance and former schoolfellow of Fred Vivian. It also chanced that he selected this evening for a call, as the Vivians stood very high socially, being an old family. Victor was rather proud of his acquaintance with them, and took occasion to call frequently.

As he was ushered into the room he did not at first recognize Frank in his new clothes.

"Victor, this is a friend of mine, Frank Kavanagh," said Fred, introducing his two visitors. "Frank, let me introduce my old schoolfellow Victor Dupont."

"We are already acquainted," said Frank. "Good-evening, Victor."

Victor stared in amusing astonishment at Frank.

"How do you happen to be here?" asked Victor, brusquely.

"By Mrs. Vivian's kind invitation," said Frank, quite at ease.

"How do you two happen to know each other?" asked Fred.

"We met in the country last summer," said Frank, finding Victor did not answer.

"I suppose you had a very good time together," said Mrs. Vivian.

"Our acquaintance was very slight," said Victor, superciliously.

"We must have gone fishing together at least a dozen times," said Frank, quietly.

"How in the world did the fellow thrust himself in here?" said Victor to himself. "They can't know his low position."

In the amiable desire of enlightening the Vivians Victor took an early opportunity to draw Fred aside.

"Have you known Frank Kavanagh long?" he asked.

"Not very long."

"Do you know that he is a telegraph boy?"

"Oh, yes," answered Fred, smiling.

"He used to be a newsboy, and sell papers in the lower part of the city."

"I didn't know that," said Fred, indifferently.

"I must say that I am rather surprised to see him here."

"Why?" asked Fred, with provoking calmness.

"Oh, you know, he is much below us in a social point of view."

"I know that he is a poor boy; but some of our most prominent men were once poor boys."

"I don't believe in mixing up different ranks."

"You didn't think so in the country last summer."

"Oh, well, a fellow must have some company, and there was no better to be had."

"You will probably be surprised to hear that your old acquaintance is to live here while I am in the country. I am going away to-morrow to spend a few weeks with my cousin."

"Is it possible!" exclaimed Victor, in surprise and annoyance. "Perhaps he is to be here as an errand boy?" he suggested, evidently relieved by the idea.

"Oh, no; he will be treated in all respects as one of the family."

"Hadn't you better tell your mother that he was once a newsboy? She might recall the invitation."

"It would make no difference with her. It seems to me, Victor, you are prejudiced against Frank."

"No, I am not; but I like to see newsboys and telegraph messengers keep their place."

"So do I. I hope Frank will keep his place till he can find a better one."

"That isn't what I meant. How can you associate with such a boy on an equality?"

"Because he seems well-bred and gentlemanly."

"I don't believe he gets more than three or four dollars a week," said Victor, contemptuously.

"Then I really hope his wages will soon be increased."

Victor saw that he could do Frank no harm, and was forced, out of policy, to treat our hero with more politeness than he wished.

When Frank rose to go, Mrs. Vivian desired him to

send round his trunk, and take possession of his room the next day.

"She doesn't suspect that I never owned a trunk," thought Frank. "I will buy one to-morrow, though I haven't got much to put in it."

CHAPTER XV

AT WALLACK'S THEATER

The next day Frank devoted what small leisure he had to the purchase of a trunk, in which he stored his small supply of clothing, leaving out, however, the clothes in which he made his first appearance in the city. These he gave to his friend, Dick Rafferty, to whom they were a welcome gift, being considerably better than those he usually wore. Dick might, out of his earnings, have dressed better, but when he had any extra money it went for some kind of amusement. He was one of the steadiest patrons of the Old Bowery, and was often to be seen in the gallery of other places of amusement. He was surprised to hear of Frank's intended removal from the lodging-house.

"I say, Frank," he said, "you're gettin' on fast. Here you are, goin' to live in a tiptop house up-town. You'll be a reg'lar swell."

"I hope not, Dick. I don't like swells very much."

"You won't notice your old friends bimeby."

"That shows you don't know me, Dick. I shall be glad to notice you whenever we meet."

"I don't see why I can't be in luck, too," said Dick. "I wish I could find some rich lady to give me a room in her house."

"You'll have to get some new clothes first, Dick."

"I know I ain't got a genteel look," said Dick, surveying his well-worn clothes, soiled and ragged; " but it wouldn't be no use if I was to dress in velvet."

" Unless you kept your face clean," suggested Frank.

" A feller can't be washin' his face all the time," said Dick.

" It's the fashion to have a clean face in good society," said Frank, smiling.

" It must be a good deal of trouble," said Dick. " Is my face very dirty?"

" Not very. There's a black spot on each cheek, and one on the side of your nose, and your chin looks a little shady."

" A feller can't keep very clean in my business."

" I suppose it is rather hard," Frank admitted; " but you won't be a boot-black always, I hope."

" I'd just as lieves give it up for bankin', or cashier of a savings-bank," said Dick. " Them's light, genteel kinds of business, and don't dirty the hands."

" Well, Dick, if I hear of an opening in either line I'll let you know. Now I must go and buy a trunk."

" I never expect to get as far as a trunk," said Dick. " I shall feel like a gentleman when I can set up one. It wouldn't be no use to me now. I'd have to stuff it with rocks to make a show."

" Poor Dick!" thought Frank as he left his friend. " He takes the world too easy. He hasn't any ambition, or he wouldn't be content to keep on blacking boots when there are so many better ways of making a living. If I ever get a chance to give him a lift I will. He ain't much to look at, but he's a good-hearted boy, and would put himself to a good deal of trouble to do me a favor."

It was not much trouble to pack his trunk. Indeed, he had scarcely enough clothing to fill it one third full.

" I may have to adopt Dick's plan, and fill it with rocks," said Frank to himself. " Some day I shall be better supplied. I can't expect to get on too fast."

6 cc   6

The room assigned to Frank was a small one; but it was neatly furnished, and provided with a closet. The bed, with its clean white spread, looked very tempting, and Frank enjoyed the prospect of the privacy he would have in a room devoted to his sole use. At the lodging-house, though his bed was comfortable, there were sixty to eighty boys who slept in the same room, and of course he had no more rights than any other.

"I hope you like your room, Frank," said Mrs. Vivian.

"It is the best I ever had," he replied.

"How early are you obliged to be on duty?" she asked.

"At eight o'clock."

"I do not breakfast till that hour; but I will direct the cook to have a cup of coffee and some breakfast ready for you at seven."

"Am I to take my meals here?" asked Frank, in surprise.

"Certainly. Did you think I was going to send you out to a restaurant?" inquired Mrs. Vivian, smiling.

"I am very much obliged to you; but I am afraid it will inconvenience the cook to get me an early breakfast."

"I am glad to see you so considerate of others. I can answer for Mary, however, who is very obliging. You can get lunch outside, as I suppose it will be inconvenient for you to leave your duties to come so far as Thirty-eighth street."

"You are very kind to me, Mrs. Vivian," said Frank, gratefully.

"I shall claim an occasional service of you in return," said Mrs. Vivian.

"I hope you will," said Frank, promptly.

Two days after he had taken up his residence in his new quarters Frank was called upon to render a very agreeable service.

"I have two tickets for Wallack's theater for this evening," said Mrs. Vivian. "Will it be agreeable for you to accompany me?"

"I should like it very much."

"Then you shall be my escort. When Fred is at home he goes with me; but now I must depend on you. Have you a pair of kid gloves?"

Frank was obliged to confess that he had not. In fact, he had never owned a pair in his life.

"I will give you a pair of mine. Probably there is little difference in the size of our hands."

This proved to be true.

Somehow Frank in his new life seemed always running across Victor Dupont. That young gentleman and his sister sat in the row behind Mrs. Vivian and her youthful escort, but did not immediately become aware of it.

"Why, Victor," said his sister, who had been looking about her, "there is Mrs. Vivian in the next row. Who is that nice-looking boy with her? It can't be Fred, for he is larger."

Victor turned his glance in the direction of Mrs. Vivian. His surprise and disgust were about equal when he saw the country boy he had looked down upon, faultlessly attired, with neat-fitting gloves, and a rose in his buttonhole and looking like a gentleman.

"I never saw such cheek!" he exclaimed, in disgust.

"What do you mean, Victor?" asked his sister, looking puzzled.

"Do you want to know who that boy is with Mrs. Vivian?"

"Yes; he is very nice-looking."

"Then you can marry him if you like. That boy is a telegraph messenger. I used to know him in the country. A few weeks ago he was selling papers in front of the Astor House."

"You don't say so!" ejaculated Flora Dupont. "Aren't you mistaken?"

"I guess not. I know him as well as I know you."

"He is a good-looking boy, at any rate," said Flora, who was less snobbish than her brother.

"I can't see it," said Victor, annoyed. "He looks to me very common and vulgar. I don't see how Mrs. Vivian can be willing to appear with him at a fashionable theater like this."

"It's a pity he is a telegraph boy, he is so nice-looking."

Just then Frank, turning, recognized Victor and bowed. Victor could not afford not to recognize Mrs. Vivian's escort, and bowed in return.

But Victor was not the only one of Frank's acquaintances who recognized him that evening. In the upper gallery sat Dick Rafferty and Micky Shea, late fellow-boarders at the lodging-house. It was not often that these young gentlemen patronized Wallack's, for even a gallery ticket there was high-priced; but both wanted to see the popular play of "Ours," and had managed to scrape together fifty cents each.

"Dick," said Micky, suddenly, "there's Frank Kavanagh down near the stage, in an orchestra seat."

"So he is," said Dick. "Ain't he dressed splendid though, wid kid gloves on and a flower in his button-hole, and an elegant lady beside him? See, she's whisperin' to him now. Who'd think he used to kape company wid the likes of us?"

"Frank's up in the world. He's a reg'lar swell now."

"And it's I that am glad of it. He's a good fellow, Frank is, and he won't turn his back on us."

This was proved later in the evening, for, as Frank left the theater with Mrs. Vivian, he espied his two old friends standing outside, and bowed with a pleasant smile, much to the gratification of the two street boys, who were disposed to look upon their old friend as one of the aristocracy.

CHAPTER XVI

FRANK AS A DETECTIVE

OF course Frank's daily duties were for the most part of a commonplace character. They were more varied, to be sure, than those of an errand-boy, or shop-boy, but even a telegraph messenger does not have an adventure every day. Twice in the next three weeks our hero was summoned by Mrs. Leroy to give her pet dog an airing. It was not hard work, but Frank did not fancy it, though he never failed to receive a handsome fee from the mistress of Fido.

One day Frank was summoned to a fashionable boarding-house in a side street above the Fifth Avenue Hotel. On presenting himself, the servant said, "It's one of the boarders wants you. Stay here, and I'll let him know you've come."

"All right!" said Frank.

"Come right up," said the girl, directly after, speaking from the upper landing.

Frank ascended the stairs, and entered a room on the second floor. A gentleman, partially bald, with a rim of red hair around the bare central spot, sat in a chair by the window, reading a morning paper.

"So you're the telegraph boy, are you?" he said.

"Yes, sir."

"You are honest, eh?"

"I hope so, sir."

"Because I am going to trust you with a considerable sum of money."

"It will be safe, sir."

"I want you to do some shopping for me. Are you ever employed in that way?"

"I was once, sir."

"Let me see—I want some linen handkerchiefs and some collars. Are you a judge of those articles?"

"Not particularly."

"However, I suppose you know a collar from a pair of cuffs, and a handkerchief from a towel," said the stranger, petulantly.

"I rather think I can tell them apart," said Frank.

"Now let me see how many I want," said the stranger, reflectively. "I think half-a-dozen handkerchiefs will do."

"How high shall I go?" asked Frank.

"You ought to get them for fifty cents apiece, I should think."

"Yes, sir, I can get them for that."

"And the collars—well, half-a-dozen will do. Get them of good quality, size 15, and pay whatever is asked."

"Yes, sir; do you want anything more?"

"I think not, this morning. I have a headache, or I would go out myself," explained the stranger. "I live up the Hudson, and I must go home this afternoon by the boat."

"Do you want me to buy the articles at any particular store?" inquired Frank.

"No; I leave that to your judgment. A large store is likely to have a better assortment, I suppose."

"Very well, sir."

"Come back as soon as you can, that's all."

"You haven't given me the money yet, sir," said Frank.

"Oh, I beg pardon! That is an important omission."

The stranger drew out a pocket-book, which appeared to be well filled, and extracted two bills of twenty dollars each, which he passed to Frank.

"This is too much, sir," said the telegraph boy. "One of these bills will be much more than sufficient."

"Never mind. I should like to have them both changed. You can buy the articles at different places, as this will give you a chance to get change for both."

"I can get them changed at a bank, sir."

"No," said the stranger, hastily, "I would rather you would pay them for goods. Shopkeepers are bound to change bills for a customer."

"I don't see what difference it makes to you as long as they are changed," thought Frank. However, it was not his business to question his employer's decision.

Sixth avenue was not far distant, and as Frank was left to his own choice he betook himself hither on his shopping tour. Entering a large retail store, he inquired for gentlemen's linen handkerchiefs.

"Large or small?" asked the girl in attendance.

"Large, I should think."

He was shown some of good quality, at fifty cents.

"I think they will do," said Frank, after examination. "I will take half-a-dozen."

So saying he drew out one of the twenty-dollar bills.

"Cash!" called the saleswoman, tapping on the counter with her pencil.

Several small boys were flitting about the store in the service of customers. One of them made his appearance.

"Have you nothing smaller?" asked the girl, noticing the denomination of the bill.

"No," answered Frank.

She put the bill between the leaves of a small blank book, and handed both that and the goods to the boy.

Frank sat down on a stool by the counter to wait.

Presently the cash-boy came back, and the proprietor of the store with him. He was a portly man, with a loud voice and an air of authority. To him the cash-boy pointed out Frank.

"Are you the purchaser of these handkerchiefs?" he asked.

"Yes, sir," answered Frank, rather surprised at the question.

"And did you offer this twenty-dollar bill in payment?"

" Yes, sir."

" Where did you get it? Think well," said the trader, sternly.

" What is the matter? Isn't the bill a good one? " asked Frank.

" You have not answered my question. However, I will answer yours. The bill is a counterfeit."

Frank looked surprised, and he understood at a flash why he had been trusted with two of these bills when one would answer.

" I have nothing to do with that," said the telegraph boy. " I was sent out to buy some articles, and this money was given me to pay for them."

" Have you got any other money of this description? " asked the trader, suspiciously.

" Yes," answered Frank, readily. " I have another twenty."

" Let me see it."

" Certainly. I should like to know whether that is bad, too."

The other twenty proved to be a facsimile of the first.

" I must know where you got this money," said the merchant. " You may be in the service of counterfeiters."

" You might know, from my uniform, that I am not," said Frank, indignantly. " I once lost a place because I would not pass counterfeit money."

" I have a detective here. You must lead him to the man who supplied you with the money."

" I am quite willing to do it," said our hero. " He wanted to make a tool of me. If I can put him into the hands of the law, I will."

" That boy is all right," said a gentleman standing by. " The rogue was quite ingenious in trying to work off his bad money through a telegraph messenger."

" What is the appearance of this man? " asked the detective as they walked along.

"Rather a reddish face, and partly bald."

"What is the color of the hair he has?"

"Red."

"Very good. It ought to be easy to know him by that description."

"I should know him at once," said Frank, promptly.

"If he has not changed his appearance. It is easy to do that, and these fellows understand it well."

Reaching the house, Frank rang the bell, the detective sauntering along on the opposite side of the street.

"Is Mr. Stanley at home?" asked Frank.

"I will see."

The girl came down directly, with the information that Mr. Stanley had gone out.

"That is queer," said Frank. "He told me to come right back. He said he had a headache, too, and did not want to go out."

As he spoke, his glance rested on a man who was lounging at the corner. This man had black hair, and a full black beard. By chance, Frank's eye fell upon his right hand, and with a start he recognized a large ring with a sparkling diamond, real or imitation. This ring he had last seen on Mr. Stanley's hand. He crossed the street in a quiet, indifferent manner, and imparted his suspicions to the detective.

"Good!" said the latter; "you are a smart boy."

He approached the man alluded to, who, confident in his disguise, did not budge, and, placing his hand on his shoulder, said, "Mr. Stanley, I believe."

"You are mistaken," said the man, shrugging his shoulders in a nonchalant way, with a foreign accent, "I am M. Lavalette. I do not know your M. Stanley."

"I am afraid you are forgetful, monsieur. I beg pardon, but do you wear a wig?" and with a quick movement he removed the stranger's hat, and, dislodging his black wig, displayed the rim of red hair.

"This is an outrage!" said the rogue, angrily; "I will have you arrested, monsieur."

"I will give you a chance, for here is an officer," said the detective.

"I give this man in charge for passing counterfeit money," said the detective. "The next time, Mr. Stanley, don't select so smart a telegraph boy. He recognized you, in spite of your disguise, by the ring upon your finger."

The rogue angrily drew the ring from his finger, and threw it on the sidewalk.

"Curse the ring!" he said. "It has betrayed me."

It only remains to add that Stanley was convicted through Frank's testimony. He proved to be an old offender, and the chief of a gang of counterfeiters.

CHAPTER XVII

FRANK MEETS AN OLD ACQUAINTANCE

FRANK was more fortunate than the generality of the telegraph boys in obtaining fees from those who employed him. He was not allowed to solicit gifts, but was at liberty to accept them when offered. In one way or another he found his weekly receipts came to about seven dollars. Out of this sum he would have been able to save money, even if he had been obliged to pay all his expenses, that is by the exercise of strict economy. But, as we know, he was at no expense for room or board, with the exception of a light lunch in the middle of the day. Making a little calculation, he found that he could save about four dollars a week. As it had only been proposed to him to stay at Mrs. Vivian's while Fred was in the country, it seemed prudent to Frank to "make hay while the sun shone," and save up a little fund from which he could hereafter draw, in case it were necessary.

So when he had saved ten dollars he presented himself

at the counter of the Dime Savings-Bank, then located in Canal street, and deposited it, receiving a bank-book, which he regarded with great pride.

"I begin to feel like a capitalist," he said to himself. "I am rather better off now than I was when I led round old Mills, the blind man. I wonder how he is getting along."

As Frank entered Broadway from Canal street, by a strange coincidence he caught sight of the man of whom he had been thinking. Mills, with the same querulous, irritable expression he knew well, was making his way up Broadway, led by a boy younger than Frank.

"Pity a poor blind man!" he muttered from time to time in a whining voice.

"Look out, you young rascal, or you will have me off the sidewalk," Frank heard the blind man say; "I'll have a reckoning with you when I get home."

The boy, who was pale and slight, looked frightened.

"I couldn't help it, Mr. Mills," he said. "It was the crowd."

"You are getting careless, that's what's the matter," said Mills, harshly. "You are looking in at the shop windows, and neglect me."

"No, I am not," said the boy, in meek remonstrance.

"Don't you contradict me!" exclaimed the blind man, grasping his stick significantly. "Pity a poor blind man!"

"What an old brute he is!" thought Frank; "I will speak to him."

"How to you do, Mr. Mills?" he said, halting before the blind man.

"Who are you?" demanded Mills, quickly.

"You ought to know me; I am Frank Kavanagh, who used to go round with you."

"I have had so many boys—most of them good for nothing—that I don't remember you."

"I am the boy who wouldn't pass counterfeit money for you."

"Hush!" said the blind man apprehensively, lest some one should hear Frank. "There was some mistake about that. I remember you now. Do you want to come back? This boy doesn't attend to his business."

Frank laughed. Situated as he was now, the proposal seemed to him an excellent joke, and he was disposed to treat it as such.

"Why, the fact is, Mr. Mills, you fed me on such rich food that I shouldn't dare to go back for fear of dyspepsia."

"Or starvation," he added to himself.

"I live better now," said Mills. "I haven't had any boy since, that suited me as well as you."

"Thank you; but I am afraid it would be a long time before I got rich on the wages you would give me."

"I'll give you fifty cents a week," said Mills, "and more if I do well. You can come to-day, if you like."

"You are very kind, but I am doing better than that," said Frank.

"What are you doing—selling papers?"

"No; I have given that up. I am a telegraph boy."

"How much do you make?"

"Seven dollars last week."

"Why, you will be rich," said the blind man, enviously. "I don't think I get as much as that myself, and I have to pay a boy out of it."

His poor guide did not have the appearance of being very liberally paid.

"Then you won't come back?" said Mills, querulously.

"No, I guess not."

"Come along, boy!" said Mills, roughly, to his little guide. "Are you going to keep me here all day?"

"I thought you wanted to speak to this boy."

"Well, I have got through. He has deserted me. It

is the way of the world.   There's nobody to pity the poor, blind man."

"Here's five cents for old acquaintance' sake, Mr. Mills," said Frank, dropping a nickel into the hand of the boy who was guiding him.

"Thank you!   May you never know what it is to be blind!" said Mills, in his professional tone.

"If I am, I hope I can see as well as you," thought Frank.   "What a precious old humbug he is, and how I pity that poor boy!   If I had a chance I would give him something to save him from starvation."

Frank walked on, quite elated at the change in his circumstances which allowed him to give money in charity to the person who had once been his employer.   He would have given it more cheerfully if in his estimation the man had been more worthy.

Frank's errand took him up Broadway.   He had two or three stops to make, which made it inconvenient for him to ride.   A little way in front of him he saw a boy of fourteen, whom he recognized as an errand-boy, and a former fellow-lodger at the Newsboys' Lodging-House. He was about to hurry forward and join John Riley—for this was the boy's name—when his attention was attracted, and his suspicions aroused, by a man who accosted John. He was a man of about thirty, rather showily dressed, with a gold chain dangling from his vest.

"Johnny," he said, addressing the errand-boy, "do you want to earn ten cents?"

"I should like to," answered the boy, "but I am going on an errand, and can't spare the time."

"It won't take five minutes," said the young man.   "It is only to take this note up to Mr. Conant's room, on the fourth floor of this building."

They were standing in front of a high building occupied as offices.

The boy hesitated.

" Is there an answer? " he asked.

" No; you can come right down as soon as the letter is delivered."

" I suppose I could spare the time for that," said John Riley.

"Of course you can. It won't take you two minutes. Here is the ten cents. I'll hold your bundle for you while you run up."

" All right! " said the errand-boy, and, suspecting nothing, he surrendered his parcel, and taking the note and the dime, ran upstairs.

No sooner was he out of sight than the young man began to walk off rapidly with the bundle. It was an old trick, that has been many times played upon unsuspecting boys, and will continue to be played as long as there are knavish adventurers who prefer dishonest methods of getting a living to honest industry.

In this case, however, the rogue was destined to disappointment. It may be stated that he had been present in the dry-goods store from which the parcel came, and, knowing that the contents were valuable, had followed the boy.

No sooner did Frank understand the fellow's purpose than he pursued him, and seized him by the arm.

" What do you want of me? " demanded the rogue, roughly. " I am in a hurry and can't be detained."

" I want you to give me that bundle which you are trying to steal from my friend, John Riley."

The rogue's countenance changed.

" What do you mean? " he demanded, to gain time.

" I mean that I heard your conversation with him, and I know your game. Come back, or I will call a policeman."

The young man was sharp enough to see that he must give up his purpose.

" There, take the bundle," he said, tossing it into

Frank's arms. "I was only going for a cigar; I should have brought it back."

When John Riley came downstairs, with the letter in his hand—for he had been unable to find any man named Conant in the building—he found Frank waiting with the parcel.

"Holloa, Frank! Where's that man that sent me upstairs? I can't find Mr. Conant."

"Of course you can't. There's no such man in the building. That man was a thief; but for me he would have carried off your bundle."

"What a fool I was!" said the errand-boy. "I won't let myself be fooled again."

"Don't give up a bundle to a stranger again," said Frank. "I'm only a country boy, but I don't alloy myself to be swindled as easily as you."

"I wish that chap would come here again," said Johnny, indignantly. "But I've come out best, after all," he added, brightening up. "I've made ten cents out of him."

CHAPTER XVIII

A RICH WOMAN'S SORROW

ONE day Frank was summoned to a handsome residence on Madison avenue.

"Sit down in the parlor," said the servant, "and I will call Mrs. Graham."

As Frank looked around him, and noted the evidences of wealth in the elegant furniture and rich ornaments profusely scattered about, he thought, "How rich Mrs. Graham must be! I suppose she is very happy. I should be if I could buy everything I wanted."

It was a boy's thought, and betrayed our hero's inexperience. Even unlimited means are not sure to produce happiness, nor do handsome surroundings prove wealth.

Five minutes later an elderly lady entered the room. She was richly dressed, but her face wore a look of care and sorrow.

As she entered, Frank rose with instinctive politeness, and bowed.

"You are the telegraph boy," said the lady, inquiringly.

"Yes, ma'am."

Mrs. Graham looked at him earnestly, as if to read his character.

"I have sent for you," she said, at length, "to help me in a matter of some delicacy, and shall expect you not to speak of it, even to your employers."

"They never question me," said Frank, promptly. "You may rely upon my secrecy."

Frank's statement was correct. The business entrusted to telegraph messengers is understood to be of a confidential nature, and they are instructed to guard the secrets of those who make use of their services.

"I find it necessary to raise some money," continued the lady, apparently satisfied, "and am not at liberty, for special reasons, to call upon my husband for it. I have a diamond ring of considerable value, which I should like to have you carry, either to a jeweler or a pawnbroker, and secure what advance you can upon it."

"And I believed she had plenty of money," thought Frank, wondering.

"I will do the best I can for you, madam," said our hero.

Mrs. Graham drew from her pocket a small box, containing a diamond ring, which sparkled brilliantly in the sunshine.

"It is beautiful," said Frank, admiringly.

"Yes, it cost orginally eight hundred dollars," said the lady.

"Eight hundred dollars!" echoed Frank, in wonder.

He had heard of diamond rings, and knew they were valuable, but had no idea they were so valuable as that.

"How much do you expect to get on it?" he asked.

"Nothing near its value, of course, nor is that necessary. Two hundred dollars will be as much as I care to use, and at that rate I shall be able the sooner to redeem it. I believe I will tell you why I want the money."

"Not unless you think it best," said Frank.

"It is best, for I shall again require your services in disposing of the money."

The lady sat down on the sofa beside Frank, and told him the story which follows:

"I have two children," she said, "a daughter and a son. The son has recently graduated from college, and is now traveling in Europe. My daughter is now twenty-six years of age. She was beautiful, and our social position was such that my husband, who is a proud man, confidently anticipated that she would make a brilliant match. But at the age of nineteen Ellen fell in love with a clerk in my husband's employ. He was a young man of good appearance and character, and nothing could be said against him except that he was poor. This, however, was more than enough in Mr. Graham's eyes. When Robert Morgan asked for the hand of our daughter, my husband drove him from the house with insult, and immediately discharged him from his employ. Ellen was high-spirited, and resented this treatment of the man she loved. He soon obtained a place quite as good as the one he had lost, and one day Ellen left the house and married him. She wrote to us, excusing her action, and I would gladly have forgiven her; but her father was obdurate. He forbade my mentioning her name to him, and from that day to this he has never referred to her.

"I am now coming to the business in which you are to help me. For years my son-in-law was able to support his wife comfortably, and also the two children which in time came to them. But, a year since, he became sick, and his sickness lasted till he had spent all his savings. Now he and his poor family are living in wretched lodgings, and are in need of the common necessaries of life. It is for them I intend the money which I can secure upon this ring."

Frank could not listen without having his sympathies aroused.

"I shall be still more glad to help you," he said, "now that I know how the money is to be used."

"Thank you," said the lady. "You are a good boy, and I see that I can trust you implicitly."

She handed Frank the box, enjoining upon him to be careful not to lose it.

"It is so small that it might easily slip from your pocket," she said.

"I shall take the best care of it," said Frank. "Where would you advise me to go first?"

"I hardly know. If I wished to sell it I would carry it to Tiffany; but it was purchased there, and it might in that case come to my husband's ears. There is a pawn-broker, named Simpson, who, I hear, is one of the best of his class. You may go there first."

"How much shall I say you want on it?" asked Frank.

"Don't mention my name at all," said the lady, hastily.

"I suppose I shall have to give some name," said Frank, "in order that the ticket may be made out."

"What is your own name?"

"Frank Kavanagh."

"Have you a mother living?"

"No," said Frank, gravely.

"Then let the ticket be made out in your name."

"If you wish it."

"Shall I bring the money to you, Mrs. Graham?"

"No; my husband might be at home, and it would arouse his suspicions. At twelve o'clock I will meet you at Madison Park, at the corner opposite the Union League Club House. You can then report to me your success."

"Very well," said Frank.

He went at once to the pawnbroker mentioned by Mrs. Graham. But for his uniform he would have been questioned closely as to how he came by the ring; but telegraph boys are so often employed on similar errands that the pawnbroker showed no surprise. After a careful examination he agreed to advance two hundred dollars, and gave Frank the money and the ticket. When Frank gave his own name, he said, "That is your name, is it not?"

"Yes, sir."

"But the ring does not belong to you?"

"No; it belongs to a lady who does not wish her name known."

"It is all the same to us."

"That was easily done," thought Frank. "Now I must go and meet Mrs. Graham."

"Have you got the money?" asked Mrs. Graham, anxiously, as Frank made his appearance.

"Yes," replied Frank.

"How much?"

"The amount you asked for."

"That is well. Now I shall be able to relieve my poor daughter. I cannot bear to think of her and her poor children suffering for the lack of bread, while I am living in luxury. I wish Mr. Graham was not so unforgiving."

"Will you take the money now?" asked Frank.

"I wish you to take fifty dollars to my daughter."

"I will do so with pleasure. What is her address?"

Mrs. Graham drew out a card, on which she had penciled her daughter's address. It proved to be a tenement-house on the east side of the city, not far from Fourteenth street.

"I wish I could go myself," said Mrs. Graham, sadly; "but I do not dare to do so at present. Give Ellen this

money, with my best love; and say to her that a month
hence I will again send her the same sum. Tell her to
keep up good courage. Brighter days may be in store."

"I will be sure to remember," said Frank, in a tone
of sympathy.

The errand was to his taste; for he was about to carry
help and comfort to those who needed both.

CHAPTER XIX

A MESSENGER OF GOOD TIDINGS

THERE stands a large tenement-house on East Fourteenth street, five stories in height, and with several en-
trances. Scores of barefooted and scantily attired children
play in the halls or on the sidewalk in front, and the great
building is a human hive, holding scores of families. Some
of them, unaccustomed to live better, are tolerably content with their squalid and contracted accommodations;
but a few, reduced by gradual steps from respectability
and comfort, find their positions very hard to bear.

On the third floor three small rooms were occupied by
Mr. and Mrs. Robert Morgan, and their two children.
She was the daughter of Mrs. Graham, and had been
reared in affluence. How she had incurred her father's
displeasure has already been told. He had been taken
sick some months before, his little stock of money had
melted away, and now he was unable even to pay the small
expenses of life in a tenement-house.

Just before Frank made his appearance there was sad-
ness in the little household.

"How much money is there left, Ellen?" asked Robert
Morgan.

"Seventy-five cents," she answered, in a tone which she
tried to make cheerful.

"And our week's rent will become due to-morrow."

"I may hear from mother," suggested Mrs. Morgan.

"If you don't, I don't know what will become of us all. We shall be thrust into the street. Even this squalid home will be taken from us."

"Don't get discouraged, Robert."

"Isn't there enough to make me despondent, Ellen? I can see now that I did very wrong to marry you."

"Do you regret our marriage, then, Robert?" asked his wife.

"Only because it has brought you poverty and discomfort."

"I have not yet regretted it."

"How different a position you would have occupied if I had not dragged you down! You would still be living in luxury."

"I should not have you and these dear children."

"And will they compensate you for what has come upon you?"

"Yes," she answered, emphatically.

"You have more philosophy than I have, Ellen."

"More trust, perhaps. Do you know, Robert, I think we are on the eve of good fortune?"

"I hope so, but I see no prospects of it."

Just then there was a knock at the door.

Thinking that it might be some humble neighbor, on a borrowing expedition, Mrs. Morgan opened the door. Before her stood our hero in his uniform.

"Is this Mrs. Robert Morgan?" asked Frank.

"Yes," she answered.

"I come from your mother."

"From my mother? Robert, do you hear that?" said the poor woman, in a voice of gladness. "Here is a messenger from my mother. Didn't I tell you there was good luck in store for us?"

Mr. Morgan did not answer. He waited anxiously to hear what Frank had to communicate.

"Your mother sends you her love, and fifty dollars," continued Frank. "She hopes to call soon herself."

"Fifty dollars!" exclaimed Ellen Morgan, in delight. "It is a fortune.

"Thank Heaven!" ejaculated her husband, in great relief.

"A month hence you may expect a similar sum," said Frank. "I suppose I shall bring it. Shall I find you here?"

Ellen Morgan looked at her husband.

"No," said he. "Let us get out of this neighborhood as soon as possible. Can't you find a respectable place to-day?"

"Yes," said his wife. "I shall be glad to move. I saw some neat rooms on West Twentieth street on Monday. They will cost us but little more, and will suit us better."

"I will send my mother my new address," she said to Frank.

"Then you may send it under cover to me, and I will see that she gets it privately," said Frank, who had received instructions to that effect from Mrs. Graham.

When Frank had left the room the little household seemed quite transformed. Hope had entered, and all looked more cheerful.

"We are provided for, for two months, Robert," said his wife. "Is not that a piece of good luck?"

"Yes, indeed it is," he answered, heartily. "Before that time I can get to work again, and with health and employment I shall not need to ask favors of any one."

"I wish father were as forgiving as mother," said Ellen Morgan.

"Your father is a hard man. He will never forgive you for marrying a poor man. He would punish you by starvation."

"He is very proud," said Mrs. Morgan. "I was an

only daughter, you know, and he had set his heart upon my making a brilliant marriage."

" As you might have done."

" As I did not care to do. I preferred to make a happy marriage with the man of my choice."

" You are a good wife, Ellen."

" I hope you will always find me so, Robert."

" I should have sunk utterly if you had been like some women."

In the afternoon Mrs. Morgan went out, taking one of her children with her. She went to the rooms on West Twentieth street, and, finding them still vacant, secured them, paying a month's rent in advance, as her mother's timely gift enabled her to do. Before the next evening they were installed in their new home, and Mrs. Morgan sent a note to her mother, under cover to Frank, apprising her of the removal.

Two days later Frank received a summons to the house on Madison avenue. He obeyed, thinking he should probably be sent with some message to Mrs. Morgan.

He found Mrs. Graham in a state of nervous excitement.

" My husband has been stricken with paralysis," she said. " It is terribly sudden. He went out yesterday, apparently in vigorous health. He was brought home pale and helpless."

" Can I do anything for him or you? " asked Frank.

" Yes; you can go at once to my daughter, and summon her to her father's bedside."

Frank was surprised, remembering how obdurate Mrs. Graham had described her husband to be.

" You look surprised," she said; " but sickness often produces a great change in us. My husband's pride has given way. His affection has returned; and it is at his request that I send for Ellen."

Frank had come to feel a personal interest in the family, and he gladly set out for the modest home in West Twen-

tieth street.   He felt that it was pleasant to be a messenger
of reconciliation.

Mrs. Morgan recognized him at once, and received him
cordially.

"Do you come from my mother?" she asked.

"Yes.   She wishes you to come home at once."

"But—my father."

"Your father is very sick; and he joins in the request."

"It has come at last—the time I have looked forward
to for so long," said Ellen Morgan, clasping her hands.
"Robert, do you feel equal to looking after the children
while I am gone?"

"Yes, Ellen.   Go at once.   God grant that your father's
heart may be softened, for your sake.   For myself I am
content to live in poverty; but I don't like to see you
suffer."

"What is the matter with father?   Did my mother tell
you?"

Frank explained, and thus gave her fresh cause for
anxiety.

On reaching her father's chamber she was shocked by
his changed appearance; but her heart was gladdened by
the wan smile that lighted up his face, assuring her that
she was welcome.   From the doctor she received the assurance that her father was in no immediate danger.   Indeed, he expressed a confident hope that Mr. Graham
would rally from his present attack, and be able to go
about his business again, though caution would be required against undue excitement or fatigue.

The doctor's prediction was verified.   Mr. Graham re-
covered; but his old pride and obduracy did not come back.
He became reconciled to his son-in-law, and provided him
a well-paid position in his own mercantile establishment,
and provided rooms in the Madison avenue mansion for the
little family whom Frank had first visited in the squalid

tenement-house in Fourteenth street, and the glad voices of children made the house no longer lonely.

"You must call and see us often," said Ellen Morgan to our hero. "I shall always remember you as the messenger who brought us good tidings at the darkest hour in our fortunes. We shall always welcome you as a friend."

CHAPTER XX

A NEW JOB, AND A LETTER FROM HOME

ONE morning an elderly gentleman entered the office in which Frank was employed, and sought an interview with the superintendent.

"I want a smart boy for detective work," he said. "Have you one you can recommend?"

The superintendent cast his eyes over the line of boys, and called Frank. Our hero's recognition of the disguised counterfeiter by his ring had given him a reputation for shrewdness.

"I think this boy will suit you," he said. "Do you wish him to go with you now?"

"Yes; I may want him a week."

"Very well."

Frank accompanied the gentleman into the street.

"Have you no other clothes except this uniform?" asked Mr. Hartley.

"Yes, sir."

"Then go and put them on. Then report to me at No. — Broadway."

"All right, sir."

"It is fortunate I have a good suit," thought Frank.

He was not long in exchanging his uniform for the neat suit given him by Mr. Bowen. Thus attired, he presented himself in Mr. Hartley's counting-room. The merchant surveyed him with approval.

"You will enter my service as errand-boy," he said. "You will be sent to the post-office, the bank, and on similar errands, in order not to excite suspicion of the real object of your presence. Keep your eyes open, and I will take an opportunity of explaining to you later what I wish you to do."

Frank bowed.

"Mr. Haynes," said the merchant, calling a thin, sallow young man, "I have engaged this boy as an errand-boy. Has any one been to the post-office this morning?"

"No, sir."

"Then he will go."

Haynes regarded Frank with disfavor.

"I have a nephew who would have liked the position," he said.

"Too late now," said the merchant, curtly.

"What is your name, boy?" asked Haynes, coldly.

"Frank Kavanagh."

"How did Mr. Hartley happen to engage you?" asked the subordinate.

"A gentleman recommended me," Frank answered.

"I had already mentioned my nephew to him. I am surprised he said nothing to me about engaging a boy."

Frank said nothing, feeling no particular interest in the matter. As he was only filling temporarily the position of errand-boy, it made little difference to him whether he was acceptable to Mr. Haynes or not.

In the course of the day Mr. Hartley handed Frank a card, containing the street and number of his residence, with a penciled invitation to call that evening.

Of course Frank did so.

Seated alone with the merchant in his back parlor, the latter said, "I have invited you here because I could not speak with you freely at the store. How do you like Mr. Haynes?"

Frank was surprised at the abruptness of the question.

"I don't like him," he answered, candidly.

"Why not?"

"There is no good reason that I know of," said Frank; "but I think his manner is disagreeable."

"Our instincts are often to be trusted," said the merchant, thoughtfully. "I confess that I myself don't like Haynes, nor do I feel implicit confidence in him, though he has been eight years in the service of our house. He is outwardly very circumspect, and apparently very faithful, but there is something in his eye which I don't like."

Frank had noticed this, but Mr. Hartley's remark called fresh attention to its furtive, crafty expression.

Frank's curiosity was aroused, naturally enough. He wondered what Mr. Haynes had to do with his mission. He did not have long to wait for information.

"I will come to the point," said Mr. Hartley, after a pause. "I am an importing merchant, and deal, among other articles, in silks. During the last year I have discovered that some one is systematically robbing me, and that parts of my stock have been spirited away. The loss I have sustained is already considerable, and unless the leakage is put a stop to, I may as well give up business. You can now guess why I have engaged you. No one will suspect an errand-boy of being a detective, while a man would very probably excite distrust, and put the rogue on his guard."

Frank listened attentively to his employer.

"Do you suspect any one in particular, Mr. Hartley?" he asked.

"It must be some one in my employ," he said. "The man who, more than any other, has facilities for robbing me is the man of whom I have spoken to you."

"Mr. Haynes?"

"Yes, Mr. Haynes. He holds an important position, and enjoys special privileges. On the other hand, so far as I can learn, he lives in a sober, inexpensive way, quite within his salary, which is liberal. He is prominently connected with an up-town church, and it seems very improbable that he would be guilty of robbery, or breach of trust; yet there have been such cases before. At any rate, I cannot wholly divest myself of suspicion."

" What do you wish me to do? " asked Frank.

" To watch Mr. Haynes carefully, both in and out of the store, to ascertain whether he has any unexplained expenses, or any questionable companions. I want to know how he spends his time out of the office. It may be that the result of my investigation will be to his credit. It may be that he is all that he seems—a reputable member of the church and of society, with nothing against him but an unpleasant manner. Should this be the case, I shall be glad to correct my suspicions, and give him back my confidence. In that case, we must look elsewhere for the rogue who is robbing me."

" Have you any particular instructions to give me? " asked Frank.

" No, only to follow Haynes, and find out all you can about him. Use great care in doing it, not to arouse his or any one else's suspicion. I will find an opportunity for you to make your reports."

" Very well, sir."

When Frank got home, he found a letter awaiting him from his country home. It was in answer to one which he had written to his uncle, Deacon Pelatiah Kavanagh, in reference to a trunk which had belonged to his father.

This is the letter:

MY DEAR NEPHEW—I am glad to learn that you are making a living in the city. It is much better that you should earn your own living than to be a burden upon me, though, of course, I would not see you suffer. But a man's duty is to his own household, and my income from the farm is very small, and Hannah and I agreed that we had little to spare for others.

There is an old trunk, belonging to your deceased father, in the attic. It contains some old clothes, which may be made over for you, and so save you expense. I would use them myself, and allow you for them, but your father was a much smaller man than I, and his clothes would not fit me. I will send the trunk by express to the address which you gave me. Of course, I shall expect you to pay the express, as I have no interest in it, or its contents.

Your cousin Jonathan has left school, and is working on the farm. I feel *so* glad that he has no extravagant tastes, but inherits the careful and economical habits of his mother and myself. I am sure he will never waste or squander the little property which I hope to leave him.

"I don't believe he will," thought Frank, "for he is about as mean as his mother, and that is saying a good deal."

Your aunt and I hope that you will steer clear of the temptations of the city. Do not seek after vain amusements, but live a sober life, never spending a cent unnecessarily, and you will in time become a prosperous man. I would invite you to come and stop with us over Sunday, but for the railroad fare, which is high. It will be better to save your money, and put off the visit till you can afford it.   Your uncle,

PELATIAH KAVANAGH.

Reading this letter, it would hardly be supposed that the writer owned ten thousand dollars in stocks, bonds, and mortgages, over and above an excellent farm. Such, however, was the worldly position of the man who sent Frank to the city in quest of a living, because he could not afford to provide for him. With some men prudence is a virtue; with Deacon Pelatiah Kavanagh it was carried so far as to be a positive defect.

CHAPTER XXI

FRANK'S FIRST DISCOVERY

So far as Frank could observe, Mr. Haynes was an active, energetic salesman. He appeared to understand his duties thoroughly, and to go about them in a straightforward manner. So far as his personal habits were concerned, they seemed irreproachable. He was neatly but plainly dressed, wore no jewelry, and carried a plain silver watch, which, when new, probably did not cost over twenty dollars.

Frank had no difficulty in ascertaining where he lived. It was in a brick house, on Waverley place, very unpretentious and certainly not fashionable. In order to find out how much he paid for his accommodations Frank visited the house on pretence of being in search of board.

" We have a hall bed-room on the third floor, at five dollars a week, including board," said the landlady. " How would that suit you? "

" I may have a friend board with me," said Frank. " In that case we should need a large room. Have you any vacant? "

" There is the front room on the third floor. We would let it to two gentlemen at eleven dollars for the two."

" Isn't the back room cheaper? " inquired our hero.

" Yes; but it is occupied by a business gentleman."

" Can you tell me his name? I may be acquainted with him."

" His name is Haynes."

" How much does he pay? "

" He pays eight dollars a week, and has the room alone."

"I suppose his room is not likely to become vacant soon?"

"Oh, dear, no. He has been with us for several years. We should be sorry to lose him. Last Christmas he gave my daughter a present of a nice silk-dress pattern."

Frank was struck by this information.

"I don't believe he paid anything for the silk," thought he. "I wish I could find out."

He had learned all he cared for, and left, saying he might call again.

"His expenses seem very moderate for a man in his position," thought Frank. "I wonder if he makes any investments."

Fortune favored our hero in the prosecution of his inquiry. Keeping Haynes in sight, as was his custom, he observed that the latter, in pulling out a handkerchief from the breast-pocket of his coat, had brought with it a letter also. Frank, quickly and unobserved, picked it up, and when he was alone looked at the address. It was directed to James Haynes, at his residence in Waverley place. On the envelope was the printed address of a real-estate broker in Brooklyn.

Frank knew that there was at that time considerable speculation in Brooklyn real estate, and he examined the letter. It ran thus:

We have found a corner lot, with several lots adjoining, near Prospect Park, which may be obtained for five thousands dollars, half cash. We have no hesitation in recommending the purchase, being convinced, from the tendencies of the market, that the buyer will double his money in a comparatively short time. If you are engaged at other times, come over on Sunday afternoon, and we will show you the property. The house you purchased of us last year is worth fully a thousand dollars more than the price you gave.

"I wonder how much he gave," said Frank to himself.

The letter was signed "Henderson & Co., No. — Fulton street."

Our hero was elated by the discovery he had made, and he sought an interview with Mr. Hartley.

"Have you discovered anything?" asked the merchant, noticing the eager look of his young detective.

Without attaching especial importance to the fact, Frank answered, "I have found out that Mr. Haynes owns a house in Brooklyn."

"Indeed!" said Hartley, quickly. "But," he continued more slowly, "he might buy one with the money saved from his salary."

"He is also thinking of buying some lots near Prospect Park."

"How did you learn this?" asked the merchant, surprised.

"I would rather not tell you," said Frank, who was not quite sure whether Mr. Hartley would sanction his examination of a private letter. "You may be sure that it is true."

"Very well; I will rest contented with that assurance. I will leave you to work in your own way. Your information is important, for it seems to show that Mr. Haynes has made investments beyond his ability, if he were dependent upon his savings alone."

"That is what I thought," said Frank. "I must try to find out where he gets this extra money."

"If you do that, and prove my suspicions correct, I will make you a handsome present, besides paying the company regular rates for your services."

"Thank you, sir. I will try to earn your gifts."

CHAPTER XXII

FOLLOWING UP A CLEW

THIS is not a detective story, and I shall not, therefore, detail the steps by which our young hero succeeded in tracing out the agency of Haynes in defrauding the firm by which he was employed. It required not one week, but three, to follow out his clews, and qualify himself to make a clear and intelligible report to Mr. Hartley. He had expressly requested the merchant not to require any partial report, as it might interfere with his working unobserved. Toward the end of the third week he asked an interview with Mr. Hartley.

"Well, Frank," said the merchant, familiarly, "who is the rogue?"

"Mr. Haynes," answered our hero.

"You speak confidently," said his employer; "but surmise will not do. I want proof, or I cannot act."

"I will tell you what I have discovered," said Frank; "and I leave you to judge for yourself."

"Have you a customer in Hartford named Davis?" he asked.

"Yes; and a very good customer. He is frequent in his orders, and makes prompt payments. I wish I had more like him."

"If you had more like him you would soon be bankrupt," said Frank, quietly.

"What do you mean?" asked Mr. Hartley, in genuine surprise. "How can a customer who buys largely, and pays promptly, be undesirable?"

"Did you know that Mr. Davis is a brother-in-law of Mr. Haynes?"

"No; but even if he is I have to thank Mr. Haynes for securing me so excellent a customer."

Hartley spoke confidently, evidently believing that Frank was on the wrong tack.

8 cc   8

"I have noticed," said Frank, "that when goods are packed to go to Mr. Davis, Mr. Haynes personally superintends the packing, and employs one particular man to pack."

"What then?"

"I think he has something to conceal."

"I don't understand what he can have to conceal. If Davis is his brother-in-law, it is natural that he should feel a special interest in filling his orders."

"I shouldn't wonder if Mr. Haynes were a partner as well as a brother-in-law of Mr. Davis."

Mr. Hartley looked surprised.

"That may be true; though I don't know why you should conjecture it. Admitting that you are right, I don't know that I have any right to object. I should like it better, however, if I were frankly told by Mr. Haynes of this circumstance."

"I will tell you what I think I have discovered," continued Frank. "The cases that are shipped to Mr. Davis not only contain the goods he has ordered, but valuable silks that he has not ordered, and does not propose to pay for."

"I see, I see," exclaimed Mr. Hartley, a light dawning upon him for the first time. "I was stupid not to comprehend your meaning earlier. What warrant have you for suspecting this?"

"First, your steady losses of goods; next, the ease with which Mr. Haynes, in his position of trust, could carry out this plan. Why should he superintend the packing of Mr. Davis's goods, alone of all your customers?"

"There is weight in what you say, Frank. You are certainly an extraordinary boy. You have shown so much shrewdness that I now ask your advice. What steps shall I take to ascertain whether Mr. Haynes is really guilty of what we suspect him?"

"There is an order now being filled for Mr. Davis,"

answered Frank. "When the order is filled, can't you open the case, and find out whether the contents correspond exactly to the bill?"

"The very thing. To facilitate matters I will send Mr. Haynes to Brooklyn on a confidential errand. Fortunately there is a matter that will give me a good excuse for doing so. Go back to your post, and when Mr. Haynes appears to be at liberty send him to me."

Half an hour later Mr. Haynes entered the counting-room of his employer.

"You sent for me, sir?" he said, a little uneasily; for, when conscience accuses, the mind is always apprehensive.

"Yes, Mr. Haynes," said the merchant, in his usual tone. "Have you any objection to go to Brooklyn for me, on a confidential errand?"

"None in the world, sir," said Haynes, relieved. "I shall be glad to take the trip this fine morning. It is almost too pleasant to remain indoors."

"Thank you; I will give you your instructions, and shall be glad to have you go at once."

It is not necessary to our story that we should know the nature of the errand on which Haynes was sent. It served the purpose of getting him out of the way.

When the suspected clerk was fairly on his way Mr. Hartley went to the packing-room, and looked about him till he discovered the case addressed to

---

H. L. DAVIS & CO.,

HARTFORD, CONN.

"Open this case," said he to one of the workmen. "There was a mistake recently in sending some goods to Davis, and I wish to compare these with the bill."

"I think they are all right, sir," said the man addressed. "Mr. Haynes saw them packed."

"Mr. Haynes will not be responsible for any mistake," said Mr. Hartley. "I would rather see for myself."

The case was opened, and the merchant discovered about two hundred dollars' worth of silk, which was not included in the bill.

"Go and call Mr. Hunting," said Mr. Hartley, quietly.

Mr. Hunting filled one of the most important positions in the establishment. To him his employer explained the nature of his discovery.

"Mr. Hunting," he said, "I wish you to see and attest the fraud that has been attempted upon me. This case was packed under the special charge of Mr. Haynes."

"Is it possible that Mr. Haynes knew of this?" exclaimed his fellow-clerk.

"Davis is his brother-in-law," said Mr. Hartley, significantly.

"Has this been going on long, do you think, sir?"

"For several years, I suspect. Mr. Haynes has, no doubt, found it very profitable."

"Shall I close up the case again, sir?" asked the workman.

"Yes, but it is not to go. You may await my further orders."

The silk was taken out, and replaced in the silk department.

"So much has been saved, at least," said the merchant.

"When Mr. Haynes comes back," he said to the usher, "send him to me."

CHAPTER XXIII

BROUGHT TO BAY

MR. HAYNES had a private reason for accepting readily the commission to visit Brooklyn. It occurred to him at once that it would give him an excellent chance to call on his real-estate agent, and confer with him upon future investments. For James Haynes had the comfortable consciousness that he was a prosperous man. Month by month, and year by year, he was adding largely to his gains, and while he was still a young man he would be rich, *if all went well.*

Of course this meant if his peculations remained undiscovered. Why should they not be? He plumed himself on the skill with which he managed to rob his employer. He was no vulgar bungler to break into the store, or enter into an alliance with burglars. Not he! The property he took was carried off openly before Mr. Hartley's very eyes, and he knew nothing of it. He did not even suspect that he was being robbed. This is what Mr. Haynes thought; but, as we know, he was mistaken. Even now he was in a net; but did not know it.

After attending to Mr. Hartley's commission Haynes went to see his broker. The conversation he had with the broker was of a very encouraging character. He was congratulated upon his investments, and assured that they would pay him handsomely.

James Haynes returned from Brooklyn in a very pleasant mood.

" A year or two more of life as a clerk, and I will throw off the yoke," he said to himself. " I must be worth at least fifteen thousand dollars now, apart from any rise in the value of my investments. When I reach twenty-five thousand I will resign my position, and go to Europe. I shall than possess an income adequate to my simple wants."

" Is Mr. Hartley in the counting-room? " he asked, as he reëntered the store.

" Yes, sir, and he wishes to see you."

" Of course he wants to see me—to hear my report."

The merchant looked up as Haynes entered the counting-room.

"So you are back?" he said, gravely.

"Yes, sir; I was detained a little, but I fulfilled my commission."

"That is well."

Here Haynes made his report. Mr. Hartley listened with an abstracted air, for his thoughts were upon the defalcation of the man before him.

Finishing his statement, James Haynes turned to leave the office, but his employer called him back.

"Wait a minute, Mr. Haynes," he said, gravely. "I wish to ask you one or two questions."

"Certainly, sir."

"I believe we have transactions with a party in Hartford, with the firm-name of H. L. Davis & Co.?"

"Yes, sir," said Haynes, starting and flushing a little.

"Is Mr. Davis a relative of yours?"

"Yes, sir. I wonder where he heard that?" Haynes asked himself. "Is there any trouble? Is he behind in his payments?" inquired the clerk.

"No; he has always settled his bills with commendable promptness."

"I insisted on that," said Haynes, in a satisfied tone. "I didn't want you to lose by any connection of mine."

"And you are quite sure that I have lost nothing by Mr. Davis?" demanded the merchant, regarding Haynes intently.

The latter changed color.

"How is that possible," he inquired, "since he has met his payments promptly?"

"You have personally seen to the packing of Mr. Davis's goods, I believe, Mr. Haynes?"

"Well—generally," stammered the rather disconcerted clerk.

"At all events, you did so this morning?"

"Ye-es."

"After you started for Brooklyn, I had the case opened,

and found some patterns of silk not included in the bill."

" I suppose there was a mistake," said Haynes, turning pale.

" You think this has not happened before? "

" I am sure of it."

" Mr. Haynes," said his employer, sternly, " you may as well drop the mask of innocence. I have been robbed systematically for the last three years, and I now understand how it was done. You and Davis, between you, have plundered me in an exceedingly ingenious manner. It will go hard with you before a jury."

" You won't have me arrested! " exclaimed Haynes, his pallor indicating his dismay.

" Why should I not? "

" You could prove nothing."

" I will take my chance of that. Have you nothing more to say? "

" I—though I do not admit that your charge is correct —I am willing to make over to you the greater part of my property, to avoid the scandal of a trial."

" That will not do, Mr. Haynes. Were I to accept this upon such a ground, you could rightfully bring against me a charge of blackmail."

" What, then, are your terms? " asked Haynes, sullenly.

" You must write out a confession of your guilt, which I shall put among my private papers, and not make public unless necessary, and in addition you must make over to me property to the amount of ten thousand dollars. It will not make up my losses, but I will accept it as restitution in full."

Against this James Haynes most strongly protested, alleging that the sum demanded was far beyond the amount of his purloinings; but finally he yielded, being privately resolved to make his brother-in-law pay one-half of the forfeiture.

"You will leave my service at the end of the week, Mr. Haynes," said his employer, "and during next week you must attend to the transfer."

"How did he find out?" said Haynes to himself, as with grave face he went about the duties of the place he was so soon to leave. "If I could find out, I would have my revenge."

CHAPTER XXIV

AN OPEN ENEMY

FRANK remained with Mr. Hartley till the guilty clerk left the establishment. This was at the special request of the merchant, who did not care to let Mr. Haynes suspect who had been instrumental in bringing his guilt to light.

"I suppose you have no further use for me, now, Mr. Hartley?" said the telegraph boy.

"Not at present, Frank," said his employer, kindly.

"Then I will report for duty at the telegraph office."

"Wait a moment. You have done me a great service."

"I am glad of that, sir," answered Frank, modestly.

"You have shown uncommon shrewdness and intelligence."

Frank looked gratified, and expressed his thanks for the compliment.

"I want to make you a present, in addition to the wages which you receive from the office," said Mr. Hartley.

"Thank you, sir."

Mr. Hartley drew from his desk a five-twenty government bond, of one hundred dollars, and handed it to our hero.

"Do you mean all this for me?" asked Frank, quite overwhelmed by the magnitude of the gift.

"It is not more than you deserve. I might have given

you the money value of the bond; but I give it to you in this shape, because I hope you will keep it as an investment. It will yield you six dollars interest annually in gold. I hope the time will come when you will have more interest in the same way."

"I hope I shall, sir. I shall feel quite rich now."

"You are richer in the qualities which have won you this acknowledgment. How do you like the telegraph service?"

"Very well, sir, for the present. It is much better than being a newsboy."

"Exactly; but there are positions you would prefer?"

"Yes, sir; I would like to be in some mercantile business, where I might work my way up. In a few years I shall be too old for a telegraph boy, and then I shall be out of place."

"I will relieve your fears on that score. In six months I shall make some changes in the list of employees. When that time comes I will find a place for you."

"There is nothing I should like better, sir," said Frank, his face flushing with pleasure.

"I am satisfied that you will make a useful and intelligent clerk. Until I want you, remain where you are. The discipline of your present office will do you no harm, but will help qualify you for usefulness and success in the mercantile career."

"Thank you, sir. Now I have something to look forward to I shall work much more cheerfully."

Frank went back to the office, and resumed his ordinary duties. One day he was riding down Broadway in a stage, when be became sensible that he had attracted the attention of a gentleman sitting opposite. This led him to scan the face of the man who was observing him. He at once recognized Mr. Haynes.

The stage was not full, and the latter came over, and took a seat next to the telegraph boy.

"Isn't your name Frank Kavanagh?" he asked, abruptly.

"Yes, sir."

"Were you not for a short time in the employ of Mr. Hartley?"

"Yes," answered Frank, feeling embarrassed, for he knew that he was suspected.

"I infer from your uniform that you have left Mr. Hartley."

"Yes."

"Why did you leave him?" asked Haynes, sharply.

"Because he had no further occasion for my services. Why did *you* leave him?" asked Frank, in turn.

James Haynes colored, and looked angry. However, he answered the question.

"I have other business views," he said, briefly.

"So have I."

The next question was also of an embarrassing character.

"Were you a telegraph boy before you entered Mr. Hartley's employ?"

"I was," answered Frank.

"Were you detailed for duty there?"

Our hero thought that he had answered questions enough by this time, and signified as much to his questioner.

"If I had been," he said, "I shouldn't be permitted to inform a stranger."

"I have particular reasons for asking the question," said Haynes.

"Then you can ask Mr. Hartley, or the superintendent of my office. Good-morning, sir, I get out here."

Frank pulled the strap, and got out. But he was not rid of his questioner. Haynes got out too, and walked beside our hero.

"I believe," he said, sternly, "that you were sent for to act as a spy on me."

"What makes you think so?" asked the telegraph boy, looking him in the eye.

"There was a difficulty between Mr. Hartley and myself, occasioned by a base and groundless charge, concocted by some enemy. I believe that you had something to do with this."

"I have brought no groundless charge against any one," said Frank.

"Did you make any report to Mr. Hartley in regard to me?"

"I must refer you to Mr. Hartley for information," said Frank. "I have an errand in here;" and he entered a store in the lower part of Broadway.

"There is no doubt about it," thought Haynes.

"That boy was a spy upon me. I have learned all I cared to. I owe you a debt of gratitude for this, Frank Kavanagh, and mean to pay the debt."

When Frank came out he thought it possible that Haynes might be waiting for him; but the disgraced clerk was gone.

"I suppose he would injure me if he had a chance," thought the telegraph boy. "I won't give him the chance if I can help it."

CHAPTER XXV

WHAT THE OLD TRUNK CONTAINED

MENTION has been made of an old trunk belonging to Frank's father, which had been forwarded to him from the country by his Uncle Pelatiah. It may be mentioned here that our hero's father had been agent of a woolen mill in a large manufacturing town. For a considerable number of years he had been in receipt of a handsome salary, and had lived in good style, but still within his income. He was naturally supposed to possess a comfortable property.

His death was sudden. He was thrown from a carriage, and, striking his head upon the curb-stone, was picked up senseless, and died unconscious. Upon examining into his affairs his administrator was unable to find any property beyond what was needed to pay the few debts he left behind him. So it came about that Frank was left a penniless orphan. His Uncle Pelatiah was his nearest relative, and to him he was sent. Pelatiah Kavanagh was not a bad man, nor was he intentionally unkind; but he was very close. All his life he had denied himself, to save money; and in this he had been ably assisted by his wife, who was even closer and meaner than her husband. It may readily be supposed that it was very disagreeable to both husband and wife to have a penniless nephew thrown upon their care and protection.

"How could your brother be so thoughtless and inconsiderate as to use up all his money, and leave his son destitute? Didn't he have a handsome income?"

"Yes," said Pelatiah. "He got two thousand dollars a year, and maybe more."

"You don't say so!" ejaculated his wife. "He'd ought to have saved two-thirds of it. I declare it's scandalous for a man to waste his substance in that way."

"My brother was allus free with his money. He wasn't so keerful as you and I be."

"I should think not, indeed. We don't begin to spend half as much as he did, and now he comes upon us to support his child."

"It don't seem right," said Pelatiah.

"Right? It's outrageous!" exclaimed Mrs. Kavanagh, energetically. "I declare I have no patience with such a man. It would only be right to send this boy Frank to the poor-house."

"The neighbors would talk," protested Pelatiah, who

was half inclined to accept his wife's view, but was more sensitive to the criticism of the community in which he lived.

"Let 'em talk!" said his more independent helpmate. "It isn't right that this boy should use up the property that we have scraped together for his cousin Jonathan."

"We must keep him for a while, Hannah; but I'll get rid of him as soon I can consistently."

With this Mrs. Kavanagh had to be satisfied; but, during her nephew's stay of two months in the farm-house, she contrived to make him uncomfortable by harsh criticisms of his dead father, whom he had tenderly loved.

"You must have lived very extravagant," she said, " or your father would have left a handsome property."

"I don't think we did, Aunt Hannah."

"Your father kept a carriage—didn't he?"

"Yes; he had considerable riding to do."

"How much help did he keep?"

"Only one servant in the kitchen and a stable-boy."

"There was no need of a boy. You could have done the work in the stable."

"I was kept at school."

"Oh, of course!" sneered his aunt, "you must be brought up as a young gentleman. Our Jonathan never had any such chances, and now you're livin' on him, or about the same. I suppose you kept an extravagant table, too. What did you generally have for breakfast?"

So Aunt Hannah continued her catechising, much to Frank's discomfort. She commented severely upon the wastefulness of always having pastry for dinner.

"We can't afford it," she said, emphatically; "but then again we don't mean to have our Jonathan beholden to anybody in case your uncle and I are cast off sudden. What did you have for dinner on Sunday?"

"Meat and pudding and ice-cream—that is, in warm weather."

"Ice-cream!" ejaculated Aunt Hannah, holding up both hands. "No wonder your father didn't leave nothin'. Why, we don't have ice-cream more'n once a year, and now we can't afford to have it at all, since we've got another mouth to feed."

"I am sorry that you have to stint yourself on my account," replied Frank, feeling rather uncomfortable.

"I suppose it's our cross," said Mrs. Kavanagh, gloomily; "but it does seem hard that we can't profit by our prudence because of your father's wasteful extravagance."

Such remarks were very disagreeable to our young hero, and it was hard for him to hear his father so criticised. He supposed they must have lived extravagantly, since it was so constantly charged by those about him, and he felt puzzled to account for his father's leaving nothing. When, after two months, his uncle and aunt, who had deliberated upon what was best to be done, proposed to him to go to New York and try to earn his own living, he caught at the idea. He knew that he might suffer hardships in the new life that awaited him, but if he could support himself in any way he would escape from the cruel taunts to which he was now forced to listen every day. How he reached the city, and how he succeeded, my readers know. We now come to the trunk, which, some time after its reception, Frank set about examining.

He found it was filled with clothing belonging to his father. Though a part were in good condition it seemed doubtful whether they would be of much service to him. It occurred to him to examine the pockets of the coats. In one he found a common yellow envelope, bearing his father's name. Opening it, he found, to his great astonishment, that it was a certificate of railroad stock, setting forth his father's ownership of one hundred shares of the capital stock of the said railway.

Our hero was greatly excited by his discovery. This, then, was the form in which his father had invested his savings. What the shares were worth he had no idea; but he rejoiced chiefly because now he could defend his father from the charge of recklessly spending his entire income, and saving nothing. He resolved, as soon as he could find time, to visit a Wall street broker, by whom he had occasionally been employed, and inquire the value of the stock. Two days afterwards the opportunity came, and he availed himself of it at once.

" Can you tell me the value of these shares, Mr. Glynn? " he asked.

" They are quoted to-day at one hundred and ten," answered the broker, referring to a list of the day's stock quotations.

" Do you mean that each share is worth a hundred and ten dollars? " asked Frank, in excitement.

" Certainly."

" Then the whole are worth five thousand five hundred dollars? "

" Rather more; for the last semiannual dividend has not been collected. To whom do they belong? "

" They did belong to my father. Now I suppose they are mine."

" Has your father's estate been administered upon? "

" Yes; but these shares had not then been found."

" Then some legal steps will be necessary before you can take possession, and dispose of them. I will give you the address of a good lawyer, and advise you to consult him at once."

Frank did so, and the lawyer wrote to Uncle Pelatiah to acquaint him with the discovery. The news created great excitement at the farm.

" Why, Frank's a rich boy! " ejaculated Aunt Hannah.

" And my brother wasn't so foolishly extravagant as we supposed."

" That may be; but with his salary we could have saved more."

"Perhaps we might; but these shares are worth almost six thousand dollars. That's a good deal of money, Hannah."

"So it is, Pelatiah. I'll tell you what we'd better do."

"What?"

"Invite Frank to come back and board with us. He can afford to pay handsome board, and it seems better that the money should go to us than a stranger."

"Just so, Hannah. He could board with us, and go to school."

"You'd better write and invite him to come. I allus liked the boy, and if we could have afforded it, I'd have been in favor of keepin' him for nothing."

"So would I," said his uncle; and he probably believed it, though after what had happened it will be rather diffi- cult for the reader to credit it.

The letter was written, but Frank had no desire to re- turn to the old farm, and the society of his uncle's family.

"I have got used to the city," he wrote, "and have made a good many friends here. I don't know yet whether I shall take a business position, or go to school; but, if the latter, the schools here are better than in the country. I hope to come and see you before long; but, I would prefer to live in New York."

"He's gettin' uppish," said Aunt Hannah, who was considerably disappointed, for she had made up her mind just how much they could venture to charge for board, and how this would increase their annual savings.

"I suppose it's natural for a boy to prefer the city," said his uncle.

"If the boy has a chance to handle his money there won't be much of it left by the time he's twenty-one," said Aunt Hannah. "You ought to be his guardian."

"He has the right to choose his own guardian," said Uncle Pelatiah. "He'll take some city man likely."

Frank did, in fact, select the lawyer, having learned

that he was a man of high reputation for integrity. He offered it to Mr. Bowen; but that gentleman, while congratulating his young friend upon his greatly improved prospects, said that he was a man of books rather than of business, and would prefer that some other person be selected.

The next thing was to resign his place as telegraph boy.

"We are sorry to lose you," said the superintendent. "You are one of our best boys. Do you wish to go at once?"

"No, sir; I will stay till the end of the month."

"Very well. We shall be glad to have you."

Three weeks yet remained till the close of the month. It was not long, but before the time had passed Frank found himself in a very unpleasant predicament, from no fault of his own, but in consequence of the enmity of the clerk whom he had been instrumental in displacing.

CHAPTER XXVI

A TRAP, AND WHO FELL INTO IT

No one rejoiced more sincerely at Frank's good luck than Mrs. Vivian. Her interest in our hero had increased, and while at first she regarded herself as his patroness she had come now to look upon him as a member of the family. Fred had already returned, and Frank, bearing in mind that he had only been invited to remain during his absence, proposed to find another home, but Mrs. Vivian would not hear of it.

"No," she said, "Fred needs a young companion, and I prefer you to any one I know of."

As Fred was of his mother's opinion, Frank readily agreed to stay. He occupied a room adjoining the one assigned to Fred, and during his hours of leisure the two were constantly together.

"I shall be glad when you leave the telegraph office," said Fred. "Then we can be together more."

"You may get tired of me."

"If I do I will let you know."

Two days afterwards Frank was riding down-town in a Sixth avenue car. Until he had taken his seat he was not aware that James Haynes was a passenger. When a lady who sat between them got out, Haynes moved up, so as to sit next to our hero.

"I see you are still in the telegraph service," he said.

"Yes, sir," answered Frank, briefly.

"I wonder Mr. Hartley didn't offer you a permanent position in his employ," said Haynes, with a sneer. "Spies are useful sometimes."

"He may give me a position sometime," said Frank, not regarding the sneer.

"You earned it," said Haynes, unpleasantly.

"Thank you," said Frank, knowing that Haynes would be provoked by his appearing to accept the compliment in good faith.

Haynes scowled, but said no more. He drew a morning paper from his pocket, and appeared to be absorbed in reading it.

At Canal street Frank rose to leave the car. He had not yet reached the door, when Haynes sprang to his feet, followed him quickly, and, grasping him by the arm, said, "Not so fast young man! Give me back my pocket-book."

Frank was struck with amazement.

"What do you mean?" he asked, indignantly.

"I mean that you have relieved me of my pocket-book. Gentlemen," turning to his fellow-passengers, "I demand that this boy be searched."

"You can search me if you like," said Frank. "You know very well that your accusation is false."

"I shall be satisfied if you produce what is in your pockets."

"That's fair," said a passenger.

Our hero thrust his hand into his pocket. To his dismay he drew out a Russia-leather pocket-book, of which he knew nothing.

"That is my pocket-book, gentlemen," said Haynes, triumphantly. "I can tell you exactly what is in it. You will find two five-dollar bills, a two and a one. Be kind enough to examine it, sir."

The pocket-book was examined, and, of course, Haynes was correct.

Suspicious glances were directed at poor Frank. Innocent as he was, he was so overwhelmed by the suddenness of the charge, and the apparent proof of it, that he looked confused and embarrassed.

"You are beginning early, my boy," said a tall gentleman, in a white cravat—a clergyman. "It is well that you are checked in the beginning of a guilty career."

"Sir," said Frank, "I am as innocent as you are. This man is my enemy, and he must have put the pocket-book in my pocket. He threatened some time since to get me into a scrape."

"That story is rather too thin," said Haynes, looking around him with a sneer. "You won't find any one here quite verdant enough to believe it."

"There you are mistaken," said a gentleman who was seated directly opposite to Haynes and Frank. "*I* believe it."

Haynes scowled at him malignantly.

"I really don't think it very important what you believe, sir. The boy is evidently a professional thief, and you may belong to the same gang for aught I know. I propose to give him in charge to the next policeman we meet."

"Do so," said the stranger, coolly. "I shall be present at his trial, and offer some important testimony."

"Indeed!" said Haynes, uneasily. "May I ask what it is?"

"Certainly. *I saw you thrust the wallet into the boy's pocket!* Of that I am willing to make oath."

James Haynes turned pale. There was a sudden change in public opinion. It was he who now had become an object of suspicion.

"Young man," said the clergyman, solemnly, "what could have induced you to enter into such a wicked conspiracy against the poor boy?"

"Mind your own business!" said Haynes, rudely. "It is a lie."

"It is the truth," said the volunteer witness, calmly.

Here a policeman became visible from the car-window, leisurely walking his beat on the western sidewalk.

"There's a policeman," said Frank's new friend. "Call him, and have the boy arrested."

"He would be cleared by false testimony," said Haynes, sullenly. "I have my money back, and will let him go."

"Then," said the stranger, rising, and displaying the badge of a detective, "I shall arrest you on a charge of conspiracy."

Haynes was fairly caught in his own trap.

"This is a put-up job, gentlemen," he said. "Am I to be robbed first, and arrested afterwards for exposing the thief?"

He looked about him appealingly; but in vain. Public sentiment was wholly against him now.

"O you ould villain!" said a stout Irish woman, "to try to ruin the poor b'ye. Hangin's too good for you."

This was rather an extreme sentiment; but Haynes saw that he was in peril. He gave an unexpected spring, and, reaching the platform, sprang out, running up a side street.

"Do you know him?" asked the detective of Frank.

"Yes, sir."

"How do you account for his hostility to you?"

Frank briefly recounted the story already known to the reader.

"He can easily be found then."

"I hope you will not arrest him, sir," said Frank. "He has been pretty well punished already, and I don't think he will trouble me again."

"If he does, send for me," and the detective handed Frank his card and address.

"It is fortunate for me," said the telegraph boy, "that you saw him put the money in my pocket."

"You would have experienced some inconvenience; but the story you have told me would have cleared you with the jury."

"My young friend," said the clergyman, "I owe you an apology. I too hastily assumed that you were guilty."

"It looked like it, sir. You were quite justified in what you said. Mr. Haynes did not appear to relish your remarks to him," added Frank, laughing.

"His crime was greater and meaner than the one charged upon you. To steal is certainly a grave offense —yet sometimes it is prompted by necessity; but a deliberate attempt to fasten a false charge upon a fellow-creature is vastly more atrocious."

"So it is, sir," said the old Irish woman, nodding assent vigorously. "I quite agree wid your honor. It is owtracious."

The passengers smiled at the old woman's mistake; but it was clear that they agreed with her in sentiment.

Meanwhile the car had been speeding along, and was near its terminus. Frank bethought himself that he had been carried considerably beyond his destination.

He pulled the bell, and, as he got out, he said, "Thank you all for taking my part."

"We don't quite deserve that," said one of the passengers, after Frank had left the car. "I was at first of opinion that the boy was guilty."

"We have been saved from doing a great injustice," said the clergyman. "It should be a lesson to all of us not to be too hasty in our judgments."

James Haynes in his hurried exit from the car fully believed that he would be pursued and arrested. He was relieved to find his fears groundless. But he was disappointed at the failure of his scheme. He had carefully prepared it, and for several days he had been in readiness to carry it into execution whenever he should meet Frank. This morning had brought the opportunity; but it had miscarried.

"But for that cursed detective I would have carried the thing through," he muttered. "He spoiled all. I *hate* that boy!"

But, though revengeful, Haynes was prudent. He gave up the thought of injuring Frank because he saw that it would be dangerous to himself. He did not remain long in New York, but soon joined his confederate in Hartford.

CHAPTER XXVII

FRANK BECOMES A GOOD SAMARITAN

THE close of the month came, and Frank laid aside his uniform. He was a telegraph boy no more.

The superintendent shook hands with him cordially, and bade him good-by.

"Come and see us sometimes," he said. "I wish you all success. Your services have been very satisfactory, and you have gained an excellent reputation."

"Thank you, sir," said Frank. "I have tried to do my duty. Good-by, boys!"

He shook hands with all his young comrades, with whom he was very popular. They knew of his good fortune.

and were disposed to regard him as very rich.   Six thousand dollars in a boy's eyes is a fortune.

"Now you're rich, Frank, I suppose you won't notice the likes of us," said Johnny O'Connor.

"I hope you don't think as badly of me as that, Johnny," said Frank, earnestly.   "I am not rich; but, even if I were, I should always be glad to meet any of you.   If I am ever able to do a favor to any of you I will."

"I believe you, Frank," said Johnny.   "You was always a good feller."

"Where's Tom Brady?" asked Frank, looking about him.   "Is he out on an errand?"

"Tom's sick," said the superintendent.   "He's got a fever."

"It's bad for him," said Johnny, "for his mother and sister depended on Tom's wages.   Poor Tom felt bad because he had to give up work."

"Where does he live?" asked Frank, with quick sympathy.

"No. — East Fourteenth street," answered Johnny.   "I know, because I live in the same block."

"I'll go and see him."

Frank's heart was not hardened by his own prosperity. He knew what it was to be poor, and could enter into the feelings of the unfortunate telegraph boy.

Half an hour found him in front of a large tenement-house, in front of which were playing children of all ages, most of them showing in their faces that unhealthy pallor which so generally marks a tenement-house population.

"Do you know where Mrs. Brady lives?" asked Frank of a girl of twelve.

"Which Brady is it?" asked the girl.   "There's three lives here."

"It's Tom Brady's mother," answered our hero.

"Is it Tom, the telegraph boy?"

"Yes."

"I'll show you then. Tom's been sick for some time."

"I know it. I have come to see him."

"Do you know Tom?" asked the girl, in some surprise; for Frank, having laid aside his uniform, was handsomely dressed, and looked like the son of a rich man.

"Yes, Tom is a friend of mine. I am sorry he's sick."

Up two flights of rickety stairs Frank followed the girl, who halted before a door.

"That's the place," said his young guide, and disappeared down the stairs, sliding down the banisters. Young ladies in the best society do not often indulge in this amusement, but Mary Murphy knew little of etiquette or conventionality.

In answer to Frank's knock, the door was opened by Mrs. Brady, a poorly clad and care-worn woman.

"What is your wish, young gentleman?" she said.

"I've come to see Tom. How is he?"

"Do you know my Tom?" asked Mrs. Brady, in surprise.

"Yes; is he very sick?"

"The poor boy has got a fever."

"Can I see him?"

"If you'll come into such a poor place, sir. We're very poor, and now that Tom's wages is stopped I don't know how we'll get along at all."

"Better than you think, perhaps, Mrs. Brady," said Frank, cheerfully. "Why, Tom, what made you get sick?"

He had entered the room, and reached the bed on which the sick boy was lying.

Tom looked up in surprise and pleasure.

"Is it you, Frank?" he said. "I'm glad you've come to see me. But how did you find me out?"

"Johnny O'Connor told me where you lived. How long have you been sick?"

"Three days. It's rough on a poor boy like me. I ought to be earning money for my mother."

"We'll miss Tom's wages badly," said Mrs. Brady; "I can't earn much myself, and there's three of us to feed, let alone the rint."

"How did you get off, Frank?" asked Tom.

"I've left the office."

"Was this young gentleman a telegraph boy?" asked Mrs. Brady, in surprise.

"Yes," said Tom; "but he's come into a fortune, and now he won't have to work."

"I'm sure I'm glad of his good luck, and it's a great condescinsion for a rich young gentleman to come and see my Tom."

"I have come into some money, but not a fortune, Mrs. Brady," said Frank; "but it does not make me any better than when I was a poor telegraph boy."

Evidently Mrs. Brady was not of this opinion, for she carefully dusted with her apron the best chair in the room, and insisted on Frank's seating himself in it.

"Have you had a doctor, Mrs. Brady?" asked Frank.

"Yes."

"What does he say?"

"He says that Tom will be sick for three or four weeks, and I don't know what we'll do without his wages all that time."

"That's what troubles me," said Tom. "I wouldn't mind it so much if I'd get my pay reg'lar while I'm sick."

"Then you needn't be troubled, Tom," said Frank, promptly, "for you shall get it regularly."

"They won't give it to me," said Tom, incredulously.

"They won't but I will."

"Do you mean it, Frank?"

"Certainly I do. I will give you a week's pay this morning, and I will call every week, and pay you the same."

"Do you hear that, mother?" said Tom, joyfully.

"God bless you, young gentleman, for your kindness to us!" said Mrs. Brady, gratefully.

"Oh, it isn't much," said Frank; "I can spare it well enough. I have had such good luck myself that I ought to do something for those who need it."

"You're a good feller, Frank," said Tom, warmly. "I'll get well quick now. If you ever want anybody to fight for you, just call on Tom Brady."

"I generally do my own fighting, Tom," said Frank, laughing, "but I'll remember your offer. When you are well, you must come and spend an evening with me."

"I'm sure he'll be proud to do the same," said Mrs. Brady.

"I must bid you good-by, now, Tom. Keep a 'stiff upper lip,' and don't be down-hearted. We must all be sick sometimes, you know, and you'll soon be well."

"I won't be down-hearted now," said Tom, "with my wages comin' in reg'lar. Remember me to the boys, Frank."

"I will, Tom."

When Frank reached home he found a large, overgrown boy, with big red hands, and clothes of rural cut, who apparently did not know what to do with his legs and arms, waiting to see him.

It was his cousin Jonathan.

CHAPTER XXVIII

A COUNTRY COUSIN

JONATHAN was a loose-jointed, heavily built, and awkward boy of seventeen, bearing not the slightest resemblance to his cousin Frank. Still he was a relation, and our hero was glad to see him.

"How are you, Jonathan?" said Frank, cordially. "I wasn't expecting to see you. Are all well at home?"

"They're pooty smart," answered Jonathan. "I thought I'd come down and look round a little."

"I shall be glad to show you round. Where would you like to go?—to Central Park?"

"I don't care much about it," said the country cousin. "It's only a big pasture, dad say. I'd rather go round the streets. Is there any place where I can buy a few doughnuts? I feel kinder empty."

"Do you prefer doughnuts to anything else?" asked Frank, with a smile.

"I hear they're cheap—only a cent apiece," answered Jonathan, "and I calc'late five or six will be enough to fill me up."

"You needn't mind the expense, cousin; I shall pay for your dinner."

Jonathan's heavy face lighted up with satisfaction.

"I don't care if you do," he said. "I hear you've got a lot of money now, Frank."

"I shall have enough to make me comfortable, and start me in business."

"I wish I had as much money as you," said Jonathan, longingly.

"You are all right. Some time you will have more than I."

"I don't know about that. Dad keeps me awful close."

"You have all you want, don't you?"

"I've got some money in the bank," said Jonathan, "but I'd like to put in more. I never thought you'd have more money than I."

"You used to tell me I ought to go to the poor-house," said Frank, smiling.

"That's because you was livin' on dad, you know," explained Jonathan. "It wasn't fair to me, because he wouldn't have so much to leave me."

In the country Frank had not found much satisfaction in the company of his cousin, who inherited the combined meanness of both parents, and appeared to grudge poor Frank every mouthful he ate; but in the sunshine of his present prosperity he was disposed to forgive and forget.

Frank led the way to a restaurant not far away, where he allowed his cousin to order an ample dinner, which he did without scruple, since he was not to pay for it.

"It costs a sight to live in the city," he said, as he looked over the bill of fare.

"It costs something in the country, too, Jonathan."

"I wish you'd come and board with dad. He'd take you for five dollars a week, and it will cost you more in New York."

"Yes, it will cost me more here."

"Then you'll come, won't you? You'll be company for me."

Frank doubted whether Jonathan would be much company for him.

"You didn't use to think so, Jonathan."

"You couldn't pay your board then."

"Now that I can I prefer to remain in the city. I mean to go to school, and get a good education."

"How much do you have to pay for board here?"

"I can't tell what I shall have to pay. At present I am staying with friends, and pay nothing."

"Do you think they'd take me for a week the same way?" asked Jonathan, eagerly. "I'd like to stay a week first-rate if it didn't cost nothing."

"I shouldn't like to ask them; but some time I will invite you to come and pay me a visit of a week; it shall not cost you anything."

"You're a real good feller, Frank," said Jonathan, highly pleased by the invitation. "I'll come any time you send for me. It's pretty high payin' on the railroad, but I guess I can come."

Frank understood the hint, but did not feel called upon

to pay his cousin's railway fare in addition to his week's board.

"What do you think of that?" asked Jonathan, presently, displaying a huge ring on one of his red fingers.

"Is that something you have bought in the city?" asked Frank.

"Yes," answered his cousin, complacently. "I got it at a bargain."

"Did you buy it in a jewelry store?"

"No; I'll tell you how it was. I was goin' along the street, when I saw a well-dressed feller, who looked kinder anxious. He come up to me, and he said, 'Do you know any one who wants to buy a splendid gold ring cheap?' Then he told me he needed some money right off to buy vittles for his family, bein' out of work for a month. He said the ring cost him fifteen dollars, and he'd sell it for three. I wasn't goin' to pay no such price, and I finally beat him down to a dollar," said Jonathan, chuckling. "I guess that's doing pretty well for one day. He said any jeweler would pay me six or seven dollars for it."

"Then why didn't he sell it to a jeweler himself, instead of giving it to you for a dollar?"

"I never thought of that," said Jonathan, looking puzzled.

"I am afraid it is not so good a bargain as you supposed," said Frank.

Great drops of perspiration came out on Jonathan's brow.

"You don't think it's brass, do you?" he gasped.

"Here is a jewelry store. We can go in and inquire."

They entered the store, and Frank, calling attention to the ring, inquired its probable value.

"It might be worth about three cents," said the jeweler, laughing. "I hope you didn't give much more for it."

"I gave a dollar," said Jonathan, in a voice which betrayed his anguish.

"Of whom did you buy it?"

"Of a man in the street."

"Served you right, then. You should have gone to a regular jewelry store."

"The man said it cost him fifteen dollars," said Jonathan, sadly.

"I dare say. He was a professional swindler, no doubt."

"I'd like to give him a lickin'," said Jonathan, wrathfully, as they left the store.

"What would you do if you was me?" he asked of his cousin.

"Throw it away."

"I wouldn't do that. Maybe I can sell it up in the country," he said, his face brightening up.

"For how much?"

"For what I gave."

"But that would be swindling."

"No, it wouldn't. I have a right to ask as much as I gave. It's real handsome if it is brass."

"I don't think that would be quite honest, Jonathan."

"You wouldn't have me lose the dollar, would you? That would be smart."

"I would rather be honest than be smart."

Jonathan dropped the subject, but eventually he sold the ring at home for a dollar and a quarter.

CHAPTER XXIX

CONCLUSION

AFTER he had accompanied his cousin to the depot, where he took the cars for home, Frank met Victor Dupont, on Madison avenue.

"Where's your uniform?" he asked.

"I have taken it off."

" Ain't you a telegraph boy any longer? "

" No, I have left the office."

" They turned you off, I suppose," said Victor, with a sneer.

" They would like to have had me stay longer," said Frank, with a smile.

Victor shrugged his shoulders incredulously.

" Are you going back to your old business of selling papers? " he asked.

" I think not."

" What are you going to do for a living? "

" I am much obliged to you for your interest in my affairs, Victor; I don't mean to go to work at all at present—I am going to school."

" How are you going to pay your expenses, then? " asked Victor, in surprise.

" I have had some money left me."

" Is that so? How much? "

" Some thousands of dollars—enough to support me while I am getting an education."

" Who left it to you? "

" My father left it, but I have only just received it."

" You are awfully lucky," said Victor, evidently annoyed. " Are you going to live with the Vivians? "

" I don't know."

" I shouldn't think you would. It would be imposing upon them."

" Thank you for your kind advice. Won't you take me to board at your house? "

" We don't take boarders," said Victor, haughtily.

It so happened that Frank entered himself as a scholar at the school where Victor was a student, and was put in the same class. Frank at once took a higher place, and in time graduated with the highest honors, while Victor came out nearly at the foot.

Frank did remain with the Vivians; they would not

hear of his leaving them, nor would they permit him to pay any board.

"You are a companion for Fred," said Mrs. Vivian, "and you exert a good influence over him. Having your company, he does not wish to seek society outside. You must let me look upon you as one of my boys, and accept a home with us."

Against this, Frank could urge no objection. He was offered a home far more attractive than a boarding-house, which his presence made more social and attractive. Having no board to provide for, the income of his little property was abundant to supply his other wants, and, when he left school, it was unimpaired.

It was a serious question with our hero whether he would continue his studies through a collegiate course. He finally decided in the negative, and accepted a good position in the mercantile establishment of Mr. Hartley. Here he displayed such intelligence and aptitude for business that he rose rapidly, and in time acquired an interest in the firm, and will in time obtain a junior partnership. It must not be supposed that all this came without hard work. It had always been Frank's custom to discharge to the utmost of his ability the duties of any position in which he was placed. To this special trait of our hero, most of his success was owing.

Our hero had the satisfaction of giving a place to his companion in the telegraph office, Tom Brady, who was in time able to earn such a salary as raised his mother and sister above want. Frank did not forget his old street comrade, Dick Rafferty, but gave him a position as porter, Dick's education not being sufficient to qualify him for a clerkship. He even sought out old Mills, the blind man, to whom he had small reason to feel grateful; but found that the old man had suddenly died, leaving behind him, to the surprise of every one who knew him, several hundred dollars in gold and silver, which were claimed by a sister of the deceased, to whom they were most acceptable.

Here end the experiences of the Telegraph Boy. He has been favored above most of his class; but the qualities which helped him achieve success are within the reach of all. Among the busy little messengers who flit about the city, in all directions, there are some, no doubt, who will in years to come command a success and prosperity as great as our hero has attained. In a republic like our own, the boy who begins at the bottom of the ladder may in time reach the highest round.

THE END.

RIP VAN WINKLE

A POSTHUMOUS WRITING OF DIEDRICH KNICKERBOCKER

BY WASHINGTON IRVING

WHOEVER has made a voyage up the Hudson must remember the Kaatskill mountains. They are a dismembered branch of the great Appalachian family, and are seen away to the west of the river, swelling up to a noble height, and lording it over the surrounding country. Every change of season, every change of weather, indeed every hour of the day, produces some change in the magical hues and shapes of these mountains, and they are regarded by all the good wives, far and near, as perfect barometers. When the weather is fair and settled they are clothed in blue and purple, and print their bold outlines of the clear evening sky; but sometimes, when the rest of the landscape is cloudless, they will gather a hood of gray vapors about their summits, which, in the last rays of the setting sun, will glow and light up like a crown of glory.

At the foot of these fairy mountains the voyager may have descried the light smoke curling up from a village, whose shingle-roofs gleam among the trees just where the blue tints of the upland melt away into the fresh green of the nearer landscape. It is a little village of great antiquity, having been founded by some of the Dutch colonists in the early times of the province, just about the beginning of the government of the good Peter Stuyvesant (may he rest in peace!), and there were some of the houses of the original settlers standing within a few years, built of small yellow bricks brought from Holland, having latticed windows and gable fronts, surmounted with weather-cocks.

In that same village, and in one of these very houses
(which, to tell the precise truth, was sadly time-worn and
weather-beaten), there lived many years since, while the
country was yet a province of Great Britain, a simple
good-natured fellow of the name of Rip Van Winkle. He
was a descendant of the Van Winkles who figured so gal-
lantly in the chivalrous days of Peter Stuyvesant, and accompanied him to the siege of Fort Christina. He inherited,
however, but little of the martial character of his ancestors.
I have observed that he was a simple good-natured man;
he was, moreover, a kind neighbor and an obedient henpecked husband. Indeed, to the latter circumstance might
be owing that meekness of spirit which gained him such
universal popularity, for those men are most apt to be
obsequious and conciliating abroad who are under the discipline of shrews at home. Their tempers, doubtless, are
rendered pliant and malleable in the fiery furnace of domestic tribulation, and a curtain lecture is worth all the ser-
mons in the world for teaching the virtues of patience and
long-suffering. A termagant wife may, therefore, in some
respects be considered a tolerable blessing; and if so, Rip
Van Winkle was thrice blessed.

Certain it is that he was a great favorite among all
the good wives of the village, who, as usual with the
amiable sex, took his part in all family squabbles, and
never failed, whenever they talked those matters over in
their evening gossipings, to lay all the blame on Dame Van
Winkle. The children of the village, too, would shout
with joy whenever he approached. He assisted at their
sports, made their playthings, taught them to fly kites
and shoot marbles, and told them long stories of ghosts,
witches, and Indians. Whenever he went dodging about
the village he was surrounded by a troop of them hanging
on his skirts, clambering on his back, and playing a thousand tricks on him with impunity, and not a dog would
bark at him throughout the neighborhood.

The great error in Rip's composition was an insuperable
aversion to all kinds of profitable labor. It could not be
from the want of assiduity or perseverance, for he would
sit on a wet rock, with a rod as long and heavy as a Tar-
tar's lance, and fish all day without a murmur, even though
he should not be encouraged by a single nibble. He would
carry a fowling-piece on his shoulder for hours together,
trudging through woods and swamps, and up hill and
down dale, to shoot a few squirrels or wild pigeons. He
would never refuse to assist a neighbor even in the rough-
est toil, and was a foremost man at all country frolics
for husking Indian corn or building stone fences; the
women of the village, too, used to employ him to run their
errands, and to do such little odd jobs as their less obliging
husbands would not do for them. In a word, Rip was ready
to attend to anybody's business but his own; but as to
doing family duty, and keeping his farm in order, he
found it impossible.

In fact, he declared it was of no use to work on his
farm; it was the most pestilent little piece of ground in
the whole country; everything about it went wrong, and
would go wrong, in spite of him. His fences were continually falling to pieces; his cow would either go astray
or get among the cabbages; weeds were sure to grow
quicker in his fields than anywhere else; the rain always
made a point of setting in just as he had some outdoor
work to do; so that though his patrimonial estate had
dwindled away under his management, acre by acre, until
there was little more left than a mere patch of Indian corn
and potatoes, yet it was the worst-conditioned farm in the
neighborhood.

His children, too, were as ragged and wild as if they
belonged to nobody. His son Rip, an urchin begotten
in his own likeness, promised to inherit the habits, with the
old clothes, of his father. He was generally seen trooping
like a colt at his mother's heels, equipped in a pair of his

father's cast-off galligaskins, which he had much ado to hold up with one hand, as a fine lady does her train in bad weather.

Rip Van Winkle, however, was one of those happy mortals, of foolish, well-oiled dispositions, who take the world easy, eat white bread or brown, whichever can be got with least thought or trouble, and would rather starve on a penny than work for a pound. If left to himself, he would have whistled life away in perfect contentment; but his wife kept continually dinning in his ears about his idleness, his carelessness, and the ruin he was bringing on his family. Morning, noon, and night her tongue was incessantly going, and everything he said or did was sure to produce a torrent of household eloquence. Rip had but one way of replying to all lectures of the kind, and that, by frequent use, had grown into a habit. He shrugged his shoulders. shook his head, cast up his eyes, but said nothing. This, however, always provoked a fresh volley from his wife; so that he was fain to draw off his forces, and take to the outside of the house—the only side which, in truth, belongs to a henpecked husband.

Rip's sole domestic adherent was his dog Wolf, who was as much henpecked as his master; for Dame Van Winkle regarded them as companions in idleness, and even looked upon Wolf with an evil eye as the cause of his master's going so often astray. True, it is, in all points of spirit befitting an honorable dog, he was as courageous an animal as ever scoured the woods—but what courage can withstand the ever-during and all-besetting terrors of a woman's tongue? The moment Wolf entered the house his crest fell, his tail drooped to the ground or curled between his legs, he sneaked about with a gallows air, casting many a sidelong glance at Dame Van Winkle, and at the least flourish of a broomstick or ladle he would fly to the door with yelping precipitation.

Times grew worse and worse with Rip Van Winkle as

years of matrimony rolled on; a tart temper never mellows with age, and a sharp tongue is the only edge tool that grows keener with constant use. For a long while he used to console himself, when driven from home, by frequenting a kind of perpetual club of the sages, philosophers, and other idle personages of the village, which held its sessions on a bench before a small inn, designated by a rubicund portrait of his Majesty George the Third. Here they used to sit in the shade through a long lazy summer's day, talking listlessly over village gossip, or telling endless sleepy stories about nothing. But it would have been worth any statesman's money to have heard the profound discussions that sometimes took place, when by chance an old newspaper fell into their hands from some passing traveler. How solemnly they would listen to the contents, as drawled out by Derrick Van Bummel, the schoolmaster, a dapper learned little man, who was not to be daunted by the most gigantic word in the dictionary; and how sagely they would deliberate upon public events some months after they had taken place!

The opinions of this junto were completely controlled by Nicholas Vedder, a patriarch of the village, and landlord of the inn, at the door of which he took his seat from morning till night, just moving sufficiently to avoid the sun and keep in the shade of a large tree, so that the neighbors could tell the hour by his movements as accurately as by a sun-dial. It is true he was rarely heard to speak, but smoked his pipe incessantly. His adherents, however (for every great man has his adherents), perfectly understood him, and knew how to gather his opinions. When anything that was read or related displeased him, he was observed to smoke his pipe vehemently, and to send forth short, frequent, and angry puffs; but when pleased, he would inhale the smoke slowly and tranquilly, and emit it in light and placid clouds; and sometimes, taking the pipe from his mouth and letting the fragrant vapor curl about his nose, would gravely nod his head in token of perfect approbation.

From even this stronghold the unlucky Rip was at length routed by his termagant wife, who would suddenly break in upon the tranquillity of the assemblage and call the members all to naught; nor was that august personage, Nicholas Vedder himself, sacred from the daring tongue of this terrible virago, who charged him outright with encouraging her husband in habits of idleness.

Poor Rip was at last reduced almost to despair, and his only alternative to escape from the labor of the farm and clamor of his wife was to take gun in hand and stroll away into the woods. Here he would sometimes seat himself at the foot of a tree and share the contents of his wallet with Wolf, with whom he sympathized as a fellow-sufferer in persecution. "Poor Wolf," he would say, "thy mistress leads thee a dog's life of it; but never mind, my lad, whilst I live thou shalt never want a friend to stand by thee!" Wolf would wag his tail, look wistfully in his master's face, and if dogs can feel pity, I verily believe he reciprocated the sentiment with all his heart.

In a long ramble of the kind, on a fine autumnal day, Rip had unconsciously scrambled to one of the highest parts of the Kaatskill mountains. He was after his favorite sport of squirrel-shooting, and the still solitudes had echoed and re-echoed with the reports of his gun. Panting and fatigued, he threw himself, late in the afternoon, on a green knoll covered with mountain herbage that crowned the brow of a precipice. From an opening between the trees he could overlook all the lower country for many a mile of rich woodland. He saw at a distance the lordly Hudson, far, far below him, moving on its silent but majestic course, with the reflection of a purple cloud, or the sail of a lagging bark, here and there sleeping on its glassy bosom, and at last losing itself in the blue highlands.

On the other side he looked down into a deep mountain glen, wild, lonely, and shagged, the bottom filled with fragments from the impending cliffs, and scarcely lighted by the reflected rays of the setting sun. For some time Rip lay musing on this scene; evening was gradually advancing; the mountains began to throw their long blue shadows over the valleys; he saw that it would be dark long before he could reach the village, and he heaved a heavy sigh when he thought of encountering the terrors of Dame Van Winkle.

As he was about to descend, he heard a voice from a distance, hallooing: "Rip Van Winkle! Rip Van Winkle!" He looked round, but could see nothing but a crow winging its solitary flight across the mountain. He thought his fancy must have deceived him, and turned again to descend, when he heard the same cry ring through the still evening air: "Rip Van Winkle! Rip Van Winkle!"—at the same time Wolf bristled up his back, and, giving a loud growl, skulked to his master's side, looking fearfully down into the glen. Rip now felt a vague apprehension stealing over him; he looked anxiously in the same direction, and perceived a strange figure slowly toiling up the rocks, and bending under the weight of something he carried on his back. He was surprised to see any human being in this lonely and unfrequented place, but supposing it to be some one of the neighborhood in need of his assistance, he hastened down to yield it.

On nearer approach he was still more surprised at the singularity of the stranger's appearance. He was a short square-built old fellow, with thick bushy hair and a grizzled beard. His dress was of the antique Dutch fashion—a cloth jerkin strapped round the waist—several pairs of breeches, the outer one of ample volume, decorated with rows of buttons down the sides, and bunches at the knees. He bore on his shoulder a stout keg that seemed full of liquor, and made signs for Rip to approach and assist, him with the load. Though rather shy and distrustful of this new acquaintance, Rip complied with his usual alacrity, and, mutually relieving each other, they clambered up a narrow gully, apparently the dry bed of a mountain torrent. As they ascended, Rip every now and then heard long rolling peals, like distant thunder, that seemed to issue out of a deep ravine, or rather cleft, between lofty rocks, toward which their rugged path conducted. He paused for an instant, but, supposing it to be the muttering of one of those transient thunder-showers which often take place in mountain heights, he proceeded. Passing through the ravine they came to a hollow, like a small amphitheater, surrounded by perpendicular precipices, over the brinks of which impending trees shot their branches, so that you only caught glimpses of the azure sky and the bright evening cloud. During the whole time Rip and his companion had labored on in silence, for though the former marvelled greatly what could be the object of carrying a keg of liquor up this wild mountain, yet there was something strange and incomprehensible about the unknown that inspired awe and checked familiarity.

On entering the amphitheater new objects of wonder presented themselves. On a level spot in the center was a company of odd-looking personages playing at ninepins. They were dressed in a quaint outlandish fashion; some wore short doublets, others jerkins, with long knives in their belts, and most of them had enormous breeches, of similar style with that of the guide's. Their visages, too, were peculiar: one had a large head, broad face, and small piggish eyes; the face of another seemed to consist entirely of nose, and was surmounted by a white sugar-loaf hat, set off with a little red cock's tail. They all had beards, of various shapes and colors. There was one who seemed to be the commander. He was a stout old gentleman, with a weather-beaten countenance; he wore

a lace doublet, broad belt and hanger, high-crowned hat
and feather, red stockings, and high-heeled shoes, with
roses in them.   The whole group reminded Rip of the
figures in an old Flemish painting in the parlor of
Dominie Van Shaick, the village parson, and which had
been brought over from Holland at the time of the settle-
ment.

What seemed particularly odd to Rip was, that though
these folks were evidently amusing themselves, yet they
maintained the gravest faces, the most mysterious silence,
and were withal the most melancholy party of pleasure
he had ever witnessed.   Nothing interrupted the stillness
of the scene but the noise of the balls, which, whenever
they were rolled, echoed along the mountains like rumbling
peals of thunder.

As Rip and his companion approached them they suddenly desisted from their play, and stared at him with
such fixed statue-like gaze, and such strange, uncouth,
lack-luster countenances, that his heart turned within him,
and his knees smote together.   His companion now
emptied the contents of the keg into large flagons, and
made signs to him to wait upon the company.   He
obeyed with fear and trembling; they quaffed the liquor
in profound silence, and then returned to their game.

By degrees Rip's awe and apprehension subsided.   He
even ventured, when no eye was fixed upon him, to taste
the beverage, which he found had much of the flavor of
excellent Hollands.   He was naturally a thirsty soul, and
was soon tempted to repeat the draught.   One taste provoked another, and he reiterated his visits to the flagon
so often that at length his senses were overpowered, his
eyes swam in his head, his head gradually declined, and
he fell into a deep sleep.

On waking, he found himself on the green knoll whence
he had first seen the old man of the glen.   He rubbed
his eyes—it was a bright sunny morning.   The birds were

hopping and twittering among the bushes, and the eagle was wheeling aloft and breasting the pure mountain breeze. " Surely," thought Rip, " I have not slept here all night." He recalled the occurrences before he fell asleep. The strange man with a keg of liquor—the mountain ravine—the wild retreat among the rocks—the woe-begone party at nine-pins—the flagon—" Oh! that flagon! that wicked flagon!" thought Rip; " what excuse shall I make to Dame Van Winkle?"

He looked round for his gun, but in place of the clean, well-oiled fowling-piece he found an old firelock lying by him, the barrel encrusted with rust, the lock falling off, and the stock worm-eaten. He now suspected that the grave roysters of the mountain had put a trick upon him, and, having dosed him with liquor, had robbed him of his gun. Wolf, too, had disappeared, but he might have strayed away after a squirrel or partridge. He whistled after him and shouted his name, but all in vain; the echoes repeated his whistle and shout, but no dog was to be seen.

He determined to revisit the scene of the last evening's gambol, and if he met with any of the party, to demand his dog and gun. As he rose to walk he found himself stiff in the joints, and wanting in his usual activity. " These mountain beds do not agree with me," thought Rip, " and if this frolic should lay me up with a fit of the rheumatism, I shall have a blessed time with Dame Van Winkle." With some difficulty he got down into the glen. He found the gully up which he and his companion has ascended the preceding evening; but to his astonishment a mountain stream was now foaming down it, leaping from rock to rock and filling the glen with babbling murmurs. He, however, made shift to scramble up its sides, working his toilsome way through thickets of birch, sassafras, and witch-hazel, and sometimes tripped up or entangled by the wild grape-vines that twisted their

coils or tendrils from tree to tree, and spread a kind of network in his path.

At length he reached to where the ravine had opened
through the cliffs to the amphitheater; but no traces of
such opening remained. The rocks presented a high im-
penetrable wall, over which the torrent came tumbling in
a sheet of feathery foam, and fell into a broad deep basin,
black from the shadows of the surrounding forest. Here,
then, poor Rip was brought to a stand. He again called
and whistled after his dog; he was only answered by the
cawing of a flock of idle crows, sporting high in air about
a dry tree that overhung a sunny precipice; and who,
secure in their elevation, seemed to look down and scoff
at the poor man's perplexities. What was to be done?
The morning was passing away, and Rip felt famished
for want of his breakfast. He grieved to give up his
dog and his gun; he dreaded to meet his wife; but it
would not do to starve among the mountains. He shook
his head, shouldered the rusty firelock, and, with a heart
full of trouble and anxiety, turned his steps homeward.

As he approached the village he met a number of people,
but none whom he knew, which somewhat surprised him,
for he had thought himself acquainted with everyone
in the country round. Their dress, too, was of a different fashion from that to which he was accustomed.
They all stared at him with equal marks of surprise, and
whenever they cast their eyes upon him invariably stroked
their chins. The constant recurrence of this gesture induced Rip, involuntarily, to do the same, when, to his
astonishment, he found his beard had grown a foot long!

He had now entered the skirts of the village. A troop
of strange children ran at his heels, hooting after him
and pointing at his gray beard. The dogs too, not one
of which he recognized for an old acquaintance, barked
at him as he passed. The very village was altered; it
was larger and more populous. There were rows of houses

which he had never seen before, and those which had been his familiar haunts had disappeared. Strange names were over the doors—strange faces at the windows—everything was strange. His mind now misgave him; he began to doubt whether both he and the world around him were not bewitched. Surely this was his native village, which he had left but the day before. There stood the Kaatskill Mountains—there ran the silver Hudson at a distance —there was every hill and dale precisely as it had always been. Rip was sorely perplexed. "That flagon last night," thought he, "has addled my poor head sadly!"

It was with some difficulty that he found the way to his own house, which he approached with silent awe, expecting every moment to hear the shrill voice of Dame Van Winkle. He found the house gone to decay—the roof fallen in, the windows shattered, and the doors off the hinges. A half-starved dog that looked like Wolf was skulking about it. Rip called him by name, but the cur snarled, showed his teeth, and passed on. This was an unkind cut indeed. "My very dog," sighed poor Rip, "has forgotten me!"

He entered the house, which, to tell the truth, Dame Van Winkle had always kept in neat order. It was empty, forlorn, and apparently abandoned. The desolateness overcome all his connubial fears. He called loudly for his wife and chidren. The lonely chambers rang for a moment with his voice, and then all again was silence.

He now hurried forth and hastened to his old resort, the village inn—but it, too, was gone. A large rickety wooden building stood in its place, with great gaping windows, some of them broken and mended with old hats and petticoats, and over the door was painted: "The Union Hotel, by Jonathan Doolittle." Instead of the great tree that used to shelter the quiet little Dutch inn of yore, there was now reared a tall, naked pole, with something on the top that looked like a red night-cap, and from it was fluttering a flag, on which was a singular assemblage of stars and stripes—all this was strange and incomprehensible. He recognized on the sign, however, the ruby face of King George, under which he had smoked so many a peaceful pipe; but even this was singularly metamorphosed. The red coat was changed for one of blue and buff, a sword was held in the hand instead of a scepter, the head was decorated with a cocked hat, and underneath was painted in large characters: GENERAL WASHINGTON.

There was, as usual, a crowd of folks about the door, but none that Rip recollected. The very character of the people seemed changed. There was a busy, bustling, disputatious tone about it, instead of the accustomed phlegm and drowsy tranquillity. He looked in vain for the sage Nicholas Vedder, with his broad face, double chin, and fair long pipe, uttering clouds of tobacco-smoke instead of idle speeches; or Van Bummel, the schoolmaster, doling forth the contents of an ancient newspaper. In place of these a lean, bilious-looking fellow, with his pockets full of handbills, was haranguing vehemently about rights of citizens—elections—members of congress —liberty, Bunker's Hill—heroes of seventy-six—and other words, which were a perfect Babylonish jargon to the bewildered Van Winkle.

The appearance of Rip, with his long grizzled beard, his rusty fowling-piece, his uncouth dress, and an army of women and children at his heels, soon attracted the attention of the tavern politicians. They crowded round him, eying him from head to foot with great curiosity. The orator bustled up to him, and, drawing him partly aside, inquired " on which side he voted?" Rip stared in vacant stupidity. Another short but busy little fellow pulled him by the arm, and, rising on tiptoe, inquired in his ear: "Whether he was Federal or Democrat?" Rip was equally at a loss to comprehend the question; when a knowing, self-important old gentleman, in a sharp cocked hat, made his way through the crowd, putting them to the right and left with his elbows as he passed, and planting himself before Van Winkle, with one arm akimbo, the other resting on his cane, his keen eyes and sharp hat penetrating, as it were, into his very soul, demanded in an austere tone: "What brought him to the election with a gun on his shoulder and a mob at his heels, and whether he meant to breed a riot in the village?" "Alas! gentlemen," cried Rip, somewhat dismayed, "I am a poor quiet man, a native of the place, and a loyal subject of the king, God bless him!"

Here a general shout burst from the bystanders: "A tory! a tory! a spy! a refugee! hustle him! away with him!" It was with great difficulty that the self-important man in the cocked hat restored order; and, having assumed a tenfold austerity of brow, demanded again of the unknown culprit what he came there for, and whom he was seeking? The poor man humbly assured him that he meant no harm, but merely came there in search of some of his neighbors, who used to keep about the tavern.

"Well, who are they? Name them!"

Rip bethought himself a moment, and inquired: "Where's Nicholas Vedder?"

There was a silence for a little while, when an old man replied in a thin, piping voice: "Nicholas Vedder! Why, he is dead and gone these eighteen years! There was a wooden tombstone in the churchyard that used to tell all about him, but that's rotten and gone, too!"

"Where's Brom Dutcher?"

"Oh, he went off to the army in the beginning of the war! Some say he was killed at the storming of Stony Point. Others say he was drowned in a squall at the foot of Antony's Nose. I don't know—he never came back again."

"Where's Van Bummel, the schoolmaster?"

"He went off to the wars, too, was a great militia general, and is now in congress."

Rip's heart died away at hearing of these sad changes in his home and friends, and finding himself thus alone in the world. Every answer puzzled him, too, by treating of such enormous lapses of time, and of matters which he could not understand: war—congress—Stony Point. He had no courage to ask after any more friends, but cried out in despair: "Does nobody here know Rip Van Winkle?"

"Oh, Rip Van Winkle!" exclaimed two or three. "Oh, to be sure! That's Rip Van Winkle yonder, leaning against the tree."

Rip looked and beheld a precise counterpart of himself as he went up the mountain—apparently as lazy, and certainly as ragged. The poor fellow was now completely confounded. He doubted his own identity, and whether he was himself or another man. In the midst of his bewilderment the man in the cocked hat demanded who he was, and what was his name?

"God knows," exclaimed he, at his wits' end. "I'm not myself—I'm somebody else—that's me yonder—no—that's somebody else got into my shoes—I was myself last night, but I fell asleep on the mountain, and they've changed my gun, and everything's changed, and I'm changed, and I can't tell what's my name, or who I am!"

The by-standers began now to look at each other, nod, wink significantly, and tap their fingers against their foreheads. There was a whisper also about securing the gun, and keeping the old fellow from doing mischief, at the very suggestion of which the self-important man in the cocked hat retired with some precipitation. At this critical moment a fresh, comely woman pressed through the throng to get a peep at the gray-bearded man. She had a chubby child in her arms, which, frightened at his looks, began to cry. "Hush, Rip," cried she, "hush, you little fool; the old man won't hurt you." The name of the child, the air of the mother, the tone of her voice, all awakened a train of recollections in his mind. "What is your name, my good woman?" asked he.

"Judith Gardenier."

"And your father's name?"

"Ah, poor man, Rip Van Winkle was his name, but it's twenty years since he went away from home with his gun, and never has been heard of since—his dog came home without him; but whether he shot himself, or was carried away by the Indians, nobody can tell. I was then but a little girl."

Rip had but one question more to ask; but he put it with a faltering voice:

"Where's your mother?"

"Oh, she, too, had died but a short time since; she broke a blood-vessel in a fit of passion at a New England peddler."

There was a drop of comfort, at least, in this intelligence. The honest man could contain himself no longer. He caught his daughter and her child in his arms. "I am your father!" cried he. "Young Rip Van Winkle once—old Rip Van Winkle now! Does nobody know poor Rip Van Winkle?"

All stood amazed, until an old woman, tottering out from among the crowd, put her hand to her brow, and, peering under it in his face for a moment, exclaimed: "Sure enough, it is Rip Van Winkle—it is himself! Welcome home again, old neighbor! Why, where have you been these twenty long years?"

Rip's story was soon told, for the whole twenty years had been to him but as one night. The neighbors stared when they heard it; some were seen to wink at each other, and put their tongues in their cheeks, and the self-important man in the cocked hat, who when the alarm was over had returned to the field, screwed down the corners of his mouth, and shook his head, upon which there was a general shaking of the head throughout the assemblage.

It was determined, however, to take the opinion of old Peter Vanderdonk, who was seen slowly advancing up the road. He was a descendant of the historian of that name, who wrote one of the earliest accounts of the province. Peter was the most ancient inhabitant of the village, and well versed in all the wonderful events and traditions of the neighborhood. He recollected Rip at once, and corroborated his story in the most satisfactory manner. He assured the company that it was a fact, handed down from his ancestor, the historian, that the Kaatskill Mountains had always been haunted by strange beings. That it was affirmed by the great Hendrick Hudson, the first discoverer of the river and country, kept a kind of vigil there every twenty years, with his crew of the *Halfmoon;* being permitted in this way to revisit the scenes of his enterprise, and keep a guardian eye upon the river and the great city called by his name. That his father had once seen them in their old Dutch dresses playing at ninepins in a hollow of the mountain, and that he himself had heard one summer afternoon the sound of their balls like distant peals of thunder.

To make a long story short, the company broke up and returned to the more important concerns of the election. Rip's daughter took him home to live with her; she had a snug, well-furnished house, and a stout, cheery farmer for her husband, whom Rip recollected for one of the urchins that used to climb upon his back. As to Rip's son and heir, who was the ditto of himself, seen leaning against the tree, he was employed to work on the farm, but evinced a hereditary disposition to attend to anything else but his business.

Rip now resumed his old walks and habits; he soon found many of his former cronies, though all rather the worse for the wear and tear of time, and preferred making friends among the rising generation, with whom he soon grew into great favor.

Having nothing to do at home, and being arrived at that happy age when a man can be idle with impunity, he took his place once more on the bench at the inn door, and was reverenced as one of the patriarchs of the village, and a chronicle of the old times " before the war." It was some time before he could get into the regular track of gossip, or could be made to comprehend the strange events that had taken place during his torpor. How that there had been a Revolutionary War—that the country had thrown off the yoke of old England—and that, instead of being a subject of his Majesty George III, he was now a free citizen of the United States. Rip, in fact, was no politician; the changes of states and empires made but little impression on him; but there was one species of despotism under which he had long groaned, and that was petticoat government. Happily that was at an end.

He used to tell his story to every stranger that arrived at Mr. Doolittle's hotel. He was observed at first to vary on some points every time he told it, which was doubtless owing to his having so recently awaked. It at last settled down precisely to the tale I have related, and not a man, woman or child in the neighborhood but knew of it by heart. Some always pretended to doubt the reality of it, and insisted that Rip had been out of his head, and that this was one point on which he always remained flighty. The old Dutch inhabitants, however, almost universally gave it full credit. Even to this day they never hear a thunderstorm of a summer afternoon about the Kaatskill but they say Hendrick Hudson and his crew are at their game of ninepins; and it is a common wish of all henpecked husbands in the neighborhood, when life hangs heavy on their hands, that they might have a quieting draught out of Rip Van Winkle's flagon.

Note.—The foregoing tale, one would suspect, had been suggested to Mr. Knickerbocker by a little German superstition about the Emperor Frederick *der Rothbart,* and the Kypphäuser Mountain; the subjoined note, however, which he had appended to the tale, shows that it is an absolute fact, narrated with his usual fidelity:

"The story of Rip Van Winkle may seem incredible to many, but nevertheless I give it my full belief, for I know the vicinity of our old Dutch settlements to have been very subject to marvelous events and appearances. Indeed, I have heard many stranger stories than this in the villages along the Hudson, all of which were too well authenticated to admit of a doubt. I have even talked with Rip Van Winkle myself, who, when I last saw him, was a very venerable old man, and so perfectly rational and consistent on every other point that I think no conscientious person could refuse to take this into the bargain; nay, I have seen a certificate on the subject, taken before a country justice, and signed with a cross, in the justice's own handwriting. The story, therefore, is beyond the possibility of doubt.   D. K."

Postscript.—The following are traveling notes from a memorandum-book of Mr. Knickerbocker:

The Kaatsberg, or Catskill Mountains, have always been a region full of fable. The Indians considered them the abode of spirits, who influenced the weather, spreading sunshine or clouds over the landscape, and sending good or bad hunting seasons. They were ruled by an old squaw spirit, said to be their mother. She dwelt on the highest peak of the Catskills, and had charge of the doors of day and night, to open and shut them at the proper hour. She hung up the new moons in the skies, and cut up the old ones into stars. In times of drought, if properly propitiated, she would spin light summer clouds out of cobwebs and morning dew, and send them off from the crest of the mountain, flake after flake, like flakes of carded cotton, to float in the air until, dissolved by the heat of the sun, they would fall in gentle showers, causing the grass to spring, the fruits to ripen, and the corn to grow an inch an hour. If displeased, however, she would brew up clouds black as ink, sitting in the midst of them like a bottle-bellied spider in the midst of its web; and when these clouds broke, woe betide the valleys!

In old times, say the Indian traditions, there was a kind of Manitou, or Spirit, who kept about the wildest recesses of the Catskill Mountains, and took a mischievous pleasure in wreaking all kinds of evils and vexations upon the red men. Sometimes he would assume the form of a bear, a panther, or a deer; lead the bewildered hunter a weary chase through tangled forests and among ragged rocks; and then spring off with a loud ho! ho! leaving him aghast on the brink of a beetling precipice or raging torrent.

The favorite abode of this Manitou is still shown. It is a great rock or cliff on the loneliest part of the mountains, and, from the flowering vines which clamber about it, and the wild flowers which abound in its neighborhood, is known by the name of the Garden Rock. Near the foot of it is a small lake, the haunt of the solitary bittern, with water-snakes basking in the sun on the leaves of the pond-lilies which lie on the surface. This place was held in great awe by the Indians, insomuch that the boldest hunter would not pursue his game within its precincts. Once upon a time, however, a hunter, who had lost his way, penetrated to the Garden Rock, where he beheld a number of gourds placed in the crotches of trees. One of these he seized and made off with it, but in the hurry of his retreat he let it fall among the rocks, when a great stream gushed forth, which washed him away and swept him down precipices, where he was dashed to pieces, and the stream made its way to the Hudson, and continues to flow to the present day, being the identical stream known by the name of the Kaaterskill.

THE FIRST BALLOON ASCENSION

(*In France, June 5th, A.D. 1783*)

BY HATTON TURNOR

FEW problems of invention have engaged more experimenters than those of aerial navigation. The history of early experiments in this direction has a peculiar interest now, in view of the numerous recent trials by aëronauts in different countries.

On Thursday, June 5, 1783, the States of Vivarais being assembled at Annonay (37 miles from Lyons, France), Messrs. Charles and Robert Montgolfier invited them to see their new aërostatic experiment.

Imagine the surprise of the Deputies and spectators on seeing in the public square a ball 110 feet in circumference attached at its base to a wooden frame of 16 feet surface. This bag, with frame, weighed 300 lbs. and could contain 22,000 feet of vapor.

Imagine the general astonishment when the inventors announced that, as soon as it should be filled with gas—which they had a simple means of making—it would rise of itself to the clouds.

Messrs. Montgolfier proceeded to make the vapors which gradually swelled it till it assumed a beautiful form. Strong arms were required to retain it; at a given signal it was loosed, rose with rapidity, and in ten minutes attained a height of 6,000 feet. It proceeded 7,668 feet in a horizontal direction, and gently fell to the ground.

In Paris this intelligence caused a meeting of savants, who, by the advice of M. Faujas de Saint-Fond, started a public subscription for defraying the expense of making inflammable gas (hydrogen), the materials of which were expensive: one thousand pounds of iron filings and four hundred and ninety-eight pounds of sulphuric acid were consumed to fill a globular bag of varnished silk, which, for the first time was designated a ballon, or balloon, as we call it, meaning a great ball.

The filling commenced on August 23rd, in the Place des Victoires, Paris. Bulletins were published daily of its progress, but, as the crowd was found to be immense, it was moved on the night of the 26th to the Champ-de-Mars.

In the morning the Champ-de-Mars was lined with troops, every house and every avenue was crowded with anxious spectators. The discharge of a cannon at 5 P.M. was the signal for the ascent, and the globe rose.

The balloon, after remaining in the atmosphere three-quarters of an hour, fell in a field, near Gonesse, a village fifteen miles from the Champ-de-Mars. The descent was imputed to a tear in the silk.

The effect on the inhabitants of this village well illustrates that the human character is the same in all countries and ages.

After it has alighted, there is yet motion in it from the gas it still contains. A small crowd gains courage from numbers, and approaches by gradual steps, hoping meanwhile the monster will take flight. At length one bolder than the rest takes his gun, stalks carefully to within shot, fires, witnessing the monster shrink, gives a shout of triumph, and the crowd rushes in with flails and pitchforks. One tears what he thinks to be the skin, and causes a poisonous stench; again all retire. Shame, no doubt, now urges them on, and they tie the cause of alarm to a horse, who gallops across the country, tearing it to shreds.

It is no wonder, then, that the paternal government of France deemed it necessary to publish the following " *avertissement* " to the public:

" Information for the People on the Ascent of
    Balloons, or Globes, in the Air.
                    " Paris, August 27, 1783.

" The one in question has been raised in Paris this said
day, August 27, 1873, at 5 p.m., in the Champs-de-Mars.

" A discovery has been made, which the government
deems it right to make known, so that alarm be not occasioned to the people.

" On calculating the different weights of inflammable
and common air, it has been found that a balloon filled
with inflammable air will rise toward heaven till it is in
equilibrium with the surrounding air, which may not happen till it has attained a great height.

" The first experiment was made at Annonay, in Vivarais, by Messrs. Montgolfier, the inventors. A globe
formed of canvas and paper, 105 feet in circumference,
filled with inflammable air, reached an incalculated height.

" The same experiment has just been renewed at Paris
(August 27th, 5 p.m.), in presence of a great crowd. A
globe of taffeta, covered with elastic gum, thirty-six feet
in circumference, has risen from the Champs-de-Mars,
and been lost to view in the clouds, being borne in a
northeasterly direction; one cannot foresee where it will
descend.

" It is proposed to repeat these experiments on a larger
scale. Any one who shall see in the sky such a globe
(which resembles the moon in shadow) should be aware
that far from being an alarming phenomenon, it is only
a machine, made of taffeta or light canvas, covered with
paper, that cannot possibly cause any harm, and which
will some day prove serviceable to the wants of society.

" Read and approved, September 3, 1783.

                                " De Sauvigny.

" Permission for printing.

                                " Lenoir."

Balloons made of paper and gold-beater's skin were now sent up by amateurs from all places which this intelligence reached, and another ascension was made.

On September 19, 1783, the King, Queen, the Court, and innumerable people of every rank and age assembled at Versailles, Jacques Montgolfier being present to explain every particular. About one o'clock the fire was lighted, in consequence of which the machine began to swell, and in eleven minutes' time, the cords being cut, it ascended, together with a wicker cage, which was fastened to it by a rope. In this cage they had put a sheep, a cock, and a duck, which were the first animals that ever ascended into the atmosphere with an aërostatic machine. When the machine went up, its power of ascension or levity was six hundred ninety-six pounds, allowing for the cage and animals.

The machine raised itself to the height of about one thousand four hundred forty feet; and being carried by the wind, it fell gradually in the wood of Vaucresson, at the distance of ten thousand two hundred feet from Versailles, after remaining in the atmosphere only eight minutes. Two gamekeepers saw the machine fall very gently, so that it just bent the branches of the trees upon which it alighted. The long rope to which the cage was fastened, striking against the wood, was broken, and the cage came to the ground without hurting in the least the animals that were in it, so that the sheep were even found feeding.

It has been sufficiently demonstrated by experiments that little or no danger is to be apprehended by a man who ascends with such an aërostatic machine; but as no man had yet ventured in it, and, as most of the attempts at flying, or of ascending into the atmosphere, on the most plausible schemes, had from time immemorial destroyed the reputation or the lives of the adventurers, we may easily imagine and forgive the hesitation that men might express, of going up with one of those machines; and history will probably record, to the remotest posterity, the name of M. Pilatre de Rozier, who had the courage of first venturing to ascend with a machine, which in a few years hence the most timid will perhaps not hesitate to trust.

The King, aware of the difficulties, ordered that two men under sentence of death should be sent up; but Pilatre de Rozier was indignant, saying, " What! Vile criminals to have the glory of the first aërial ascension! No, not on any account!" He stirs up the city in his behalf, and the King at length yields to the earnest entreaties of the Marquis d'Arlandes, who said that he would accompany him.

Scarce ten months had elapsed since M. Montgolfier made his first aërostatic experiment, when M. Pilatre de Rozier publicly offered himself to be the first adventurer in the newly invented aërial machine. His offer was accepted, and on October 15, 1783, he actually ascended, to the astonishment of a gazing multitude. The following are the particulars of this experiment:

M. Montgolfier constructed another machine. Sufficient time was allowed for the work to be properly done; and by October 10th the aërostat was completed. It had an oval shape; its diameter being about forty-eight feet, and its height about seventy-four. The outside was elegantly painted and decorated with the signs of the zodiac, with the cipher of the King's name in *fleurs-de-lis*, etc. The aperture or lower part of the machine had a wicker gallery about three feet broad, with a balustrade both within and without about three feet high. The inner diameter of this gallery, and of the aperture of the machine, the neck of which passed through it, was near sixteen feet. In the middle of this aperture an iron grate or brazier was supported by chains which came down from the sides of the machine.

In this construction, when the machine was in the air, with a fire lighted in the grate, it was easy for a person who stood in the gallery, and had fuel with him, to keep up the fire in the mouth of the machine, by throwing the fuel on the grate through port-holes made in the neck of the machine. By this means it was expected, as it was found by experience, that the machine might be kept up as long as the person in its gallery thought proper, or while he had fuel to supply the fire. The weight of this aërostat was upwards of 16,000 pounds.

On Wednesday, October 15th, this memorable experiment was performed. The fire being lighted, and the machine inflated, M. Pilatre de Rozier placed himself in the gallery, and, after a few trials close to the ground, he desired to ascend to a great height; the machine was accordingly permitted to rise, and it ascended as high as the ropes, which were purposely placed to detain it, would allow, which was about eighty-four feet from the ground. There M. de Rozier kept the machine afloat during four minutes twenty-five seconds by throwing straw and wool into the grate to keep up the fire; then the machine descended very gently; but such was its tendency to ascend, that after touching the ground, the moment M. de Rozier came out of the gallery, it rebounded again to a considerable height. The intrepid adventurer, returning from the sky, assured his friends and the multitude that gazed on him with admiration, that he had not experienced the least inconvenience, either in going up, in remaining there, or in descending. He received the compliments due to his courage and audacity.

On October 17th, M. Pilatre de Rozier repeated the experiment with nearly the same success as he had two days before. The machine was elevated to about the same height, being still detained by ropes, but the wind being strong, it did not sustain itself so well, and consequently did not afford so fine a spectacle to the concourse of people, which at this time was much greater than at the preceding experiment.

On the Sunday following, which was the 19th, the weather proving favorable, M. Montgolfier employed his machine to make the following experiments. At half-past four o'clock the machine was filled in five minutes' time; then M. Pilatre de Rozier placed himself in the gallery, a counterpoise of one hundred pounds being put in the opposite side of it, to preserve the balance. The size of the gallery had now been diminished. The machine was permitted to ascend to the height of about two hundred and ten feet, where it remained during six minutes, not having any fire in the grate; and then it descended very gently.

Soon after, everything remaining as before, except that now a fire was put into the grate, the machine was permitted to ascend to about two hundred and sixty-two feet, where it remained stationary during eight minutes and a half. On pulling it down, a gust of wind carried it over some large trees in an adjoining garden, where it would have been in great danger had not M. de Rozier, with great presence of mind and address, increased the fire by throwing some straw upon it; by which means the machine was extricated from so dangerous a situation, and rose majestically to its former situation, amid the acclamations of the spectators. On descending, M. de Rozier threw some straw upon the fire, which made the machine ascend once more, remaining up for about the same length of time.

In consequence of the report of the foregoing experiments, signed by the commissaries of the Academy of Sciences, that learned and respectable body ordered: (1) That the said report should be printed and published; and (2) that the annual prize of six hundred livres, from the fund provided by an anonymous citizen, be given to Messrs. Montgolfier, for the year 1783.